DEAL WITH THE DEVIL

CYNTHIA EDEN

This book is a work of fiction. Any similarities to real people, places, or events are not intentional and are purely the result of coincidence. The characters, places, and events in this story are fictional.

Published by Cynthia Eden.

Cover art and design by: Sweet 'N Spicy Designs

Proof-reading by: J. R. T. Editing

CHAPTER ONE

"Do you enjoy watching me?" Ella Lancaster asked softly as she stared into the one-way mirror. Her own reflection peered back at her, but she knew he was there. Standing just on the other side of that glass. Watching her. Always, watching.

And I'm his prisoner. As if she hadn't played this particular game—or nightmare—before. Only this time, something seemed different. Was he different? Or just another man she would have to kill?

Ella lifted her hand to the glass. Her image appeared fragile. A woman—delicate, almost petite—with long, dark hair and light blue, almond-shaped eyes. Her palm flattened against the glass, almost as if she were trying to touch the man who waited on the other side.

But I'm not so interested in touching you…more interested in fighting you and escaping.

Because she couldn't stay his prisoner. She was going out of her mind being captive once again.

"No chains on my wrists," Ella said as she cocked her head. "A fancy room instead of jail bars, but I know a prison when I see one." And he could stock the place with all the high-end furniture and too expensive clothing that he wanted. She knew where she was, and there was no pretending. "I want out."

She'd already spent too much time being held captive. Her nightmare had been going on for far too long.

That sick, twisted freak of an alpha werewolf named Keegan had been the start of her most recent hell. He'd kept her chained and starved in his basement. He'd nearly broken her mind…

Nearly? She almost laughed at that thought. Ella knew her mind *was* broken. So was she.

But Keegan was gone now. And she was in the custody of the United States government. The FBI. The government was supposed to protect people, right?

It's a pity that rule doesn't apply to paranormals.

"You watch me all the time," she whispered. "Do you think I don't feel you?" She smiled at him and could see the flash of her fangs reflected in the mirror. "Is it really right for someone like you to hold me prisoner?" Ella kept her hand against the glass. "After all, you're just as much of a monster as I am."

Did he think she hadn't realized that?

"Now let me out," she said, voice soft, beguiling.

Nothing.

"Let me out!" Ella said again, voice harder. She wanted to drive her fist into that glass and shatter it. The man on the other side of that mirror had no idea just who he was dealing with. She was getting stronger now, and soon, soon everyone would be feeling her rage.

I won't be a victim again. I won't!

She strained to hear sounds from that other room. The people in power there believed they were so clever, trying to use their sound-proofing technology. They didn't know just what she could do.

Fools. *Know your enemy.* That was rule one for survival.

As she strained, Ella could hear the faint taps of footsteps. Her watcher was coming closer. Heading to her door.

She kept her hand on the glass, not moving at all even as adrenaline burst through her veins. He hadn't come to see her—not without glass between them—since she'd first been brought in.

Just watching. Day and night...*watching...*

He'd sent his team members in to poke and prod her. Sent a doctor who'd taken her blood and all kinds of test samples. The guards had been there, too, of course. But the watcher had stayed away. The man in charge.

Ella heard the click of the lock and the slide of the bolt as her cell was unlocked. *It's a cell. I don't care how much you try to pretty it up.* The door opened.

His scent hit her first. Rich, masculine. The scent seemed to wrap around her.

Tempt her.

Then he was advancing in the room. Moving with a slow, confident stride. Her gaze slid up and she saw his reflection in that mirror. Tall, fit, with shoulders that seemed incredibly wide. *Power.* That was what she noticed first about him. Long before she even focused on his face, Ella was aware of the power that his muscled body possessed.

Power equals danger.

She swallowed down her fear and made herself study his face.

She'd seen him before, of course, when she'd been pulled from her previous prison. Keegan's torture center. When she'd been rescued from the deranged werewolf who'd been determined to drain every bit of power from her body.

He had been there.

The blond male who now stood, still and silent, just a few feet away.

A handsome man, if you went for that sort. She never had. His jaw was hard, his forehead high. His nose was elegant—far too much so for her taste. It needed to be broken, maybe that would give the guy character. Maybe that would make him look less cold.

Cold. That was definitely the way she felt when she stared at him. Maybe it was his eyes. Those hard eyes of his held no hint of any emotion. And his lips—lips that *could* have been sensual—were pressed into a taut line.

This was a man who gave nothing away.

Then I suppose I'll have to take everything from him.

He was dressed in a well-cut suit, one that perfectly displayed his wide shoulders and fit his tall frame. He looked polished. Powerful. Determined.

Not your average jailer…

"Have you looked long enough?" he asked. His voice was a deep, dark rumble. Sexy.

She didn't want to find anything about her jailer to be sexy. This attraction she had to him—it was odd. Unwanted.

But…there. Instinctive. Primal. Even her heart was already beating faster, and not just because she thought escape was at hand. Because he was close, and he stirred her.

Ella lowered her hand away from the glass. She slowly turned to face him, making sure that her own expression was schooled not to show her emotions. She was going to try logic with him first. She'd plead her case. Perhaps that tactic would work.

And perhaps not.

"You've had plenty of time to *look* at me," Ella murmured. "I suppose I thought it was only fair for me to have the same opportunity."

His jaw hardened. Just a small movement, but she saw it and Ella liked that she'd gotten to him.

"Did you think I didn't know? I could feel it when you were close." She motioned toward the mirror, then toward the video camera mounted near the ceiling. "I think this was all a bit…much, don't you? I mean, I'm locked in. It's not as if I can plot some terrible wickedness here."

"You can plot it," he allowed, "you just can't carry it out."

Ella took a step closer to him.

He offered her his hand. "It's time we were officially introduced. My name is Eric Pate, and I'm in charge of the FBI's Para Unit."

She stared at his hand.

The Para Unit. There had been whispers about that group for years. Government agents who policed the creatures that went bump in the night. According to the gossip she'd heard, if a supernatural got on the wrong side of the Para Unit, well, that supernatural found his—or her—butt tossed into Purgatory.

Is Purgatory real?

Ella was very much afraid that it was.

"I don't bite," Eric murmured. His hand was still offered toward her.

"No." Ella cleared her throat. "I think that's my deal." Because she didn't want to show him her fear, she put her hand in his.

Heat.

Her breath caught in her throat. And, yes, she still breathed. Her heart still beat, she could still feel pain and pleasure. Despite the tales heard by so many, paranormals were still alive. They could hurt, they could feel…just like humans.

Ella had thought that the man before her was cold. Emotionless. After all, a darkness seemed to cling to him like a shroud, but when they touched—fire seemed to ignite in her hand. Her heart beat even faster, nearly racing out of control. Her breasts ached, as if wanting, needing a lover's touch. And—

She tried to pull away.

But his hand tightened around hers. She could feel the strength in that hand.

"Is something wrong?"

Yes, you're what's wrong! The man before her was far from human, no matter what he wanted to pretend. And she should *not* be reacting to him that way. His scent wasn't human. It was just slightly…off. Everything about him was, yet she was still feeling that pull between them.

"Let me go," she told him, keeping her voice flat by using every single drop of self-control that she possessed.

A faint smile curved his lips. That smile never reached his eyes as he—very slowly—eased his hand away from hers. Before he let her go completely, his fingers trailed over her inner wrist, right above the pulse that raced so frantically.

"I would have thought…" Eric murmured, "That you would be a bit more appreciative."

"Appreciative?" Ella nearly strangled on the word. "You've kept me locked up—"

"In the best room money can buy…"

"I haven't seen the outside world in two weeks—"

"You're a vampire," he said, frowning a bit. "I would think that me keeping you out of the sunlight would be a good thing for you. Something that you might even *thank* me for."

Think again, buddy. Sunlight did weaken most vamps. She didn't happen to share that weakness.

"I want to be released," Ella announced. "I haven't done anything wrong." Nothing he knew about, anyway. The sooner she was away from him and his Para Unit, the better. "I was a victim!"

For an instant, what could have been sympathy flashed over his face. "Yes, I believe you were."

"*Believe*?" Okay, she was repeating the guy way too much and her voice had just risen to a near ear-splitting degree. She sucked in a deep breath and tried to get her control back. Back, back, back! "I was chained in that werewolf's basement. He starved me. He tortured me." *He made me wish for death.* Only death hadn't come. Keegan James hadn't been about to let his new prize escape into the afterlife. "All I want is to be free. I am not a threat to you." Maybe. Mostly?

His gaze swept over her. Such a calculating stare. "You've been fed while you were here." A pause. "And you're certainly looking…*better*…now."

"Yes, well, considering that I looked like a walking skeleton when I was brought in, just about anything has to be an improvement." She paced over to the little table in her "kitchen" area and picked up an empty blood bag. "But this isn't exactly hitting the spot for me."

One heavy brow rose as he crossed his arms over his chest and continued to study her. "Why? Because you like to get your blood straight from the vein?"

Actually, yes, but that wasn't something she'd reveal right then. Though tapping his vein was tempting. Ella cleared her throat. "I prefer blood that hasn't been drugged."

He just stared back at her.

"Did you think I couldn't taste the drugs in it? You're trying to keep me controlled." That seriously infuriated her. "At all times. But I don't deserve that. I've done nothing to you!"

"Most vampires don't taste the drugs."

She dropped the bag back on the table and realized she'd made her first mistake. *I'm supposed to act like every other vampire. I'm not supposed to stick out.* "Well, maybe it was because I'd gone so long without the blood." *No, stop, don't give excuses. That will just draw more of his attention.* "You don't have to drug me. I'm no threat to you or anyone else."

He seemed to consider that. Then he stalked toward her, and that was the only way she could describe his movement—stalking. Graceful, dangerous, like a jungle cat after prey. She didn't want to be his prey.

His hand lifted.

She flinched.

"It's okay," Eric told her. "I'm not going to hurt you."

She didn't call him a liar. After all, she was trying to get on his good side. Freedom had a price, Ella knew that.

His hand skimmed down her cheek. It was odd—a caress. Why would her jailer be caressing her?

Her stomach knotted. "No."

He blinked those eerily compelling eyes of his. Were they blue or green? It was hard for her to tell for certain. The color seemed to keep shifting the more she stared into his gaze. At first, she'd thought they were a pure green, but the more she looked into them…

Focus, Ella.

She wanted to be clear about one thing. "I'm not going to have sex with you." Despite the insane way her body was responding to him.

His hand stilled. "Did I…ask for sex?"

"You're touching me."

"Yes."

"And you…want me."

His gaze sharpened. "Just how do you know that?"

Oh, crap…*Mistake number two.* She could pick up on his emotions—and, despite his powerful control—Ella *had* felt his desire in the air around them. But an average, run-of-the-mill vampire wasn't supposed to literally feel emotions and desires in the air. At least not without first drinking from a victim. *Donor. Donor, not victim.* "You're touching me," she whispered. "And your pupils have gone wide. I know when a man wants me."

That sounded good. She hoped.

"I didn't ask you for sex," Eric said as his hand fell away.

"Then why did you touch me?"

His head cocked to the right as he studied her. "Because…I wanted to."

"Don't do it again." She backed up a step. "I don't like being touched, all right? That hand shake? That was more than enough for me."

He nodded. "Until you ask, I won't."

What? The guy shouldn't hold his breath. He'd pass out. "I'm only asking to be let go! I'm only asking—"

"You haven't told me your name. Not me. Not anyone here."

Her laughter sounded bitter, even to her own ears. "You mean the other jailers? The guards who slip in the blood while staring at me with fear in their gazes? No, I didn't tell them my name."

He headed over to her couch and just sat down. Made himself all at home as he sprawled there, in her cell. Her perfect, fancy prison that looked like something out of the pages of a glossy home design magazine. "There's a certain way things work here."

She clasped her hands behind her back, the better for him *not* to see that her nails were sharpening into mini-claws.

"Information can buy you a whole lot..." Eric drawled.

"Can it buy freedom?"

"Perhaps."

"I don't get it!" Ella burst out. "I thought you were one of the good guys. I thought—"

"You shouldn't make that mistake." His fingers drummed against the arm of her couch. "Don't ever do that. Just because I have a badge, it doesn't necessarily mean I'm good."

She licked her lips. "What do you want from me?"

His brow furrowed as he seemed to consider that. His stare slowly traveled over her body, and she—she didn't like it. She felt too tense beneath his stare. Too nervous and—

"We'll start simply. Tell me about yourself."

That would be the *opposite* of simple, and she wasn't about to make that extreme blunder. "I'm Ella, Ella Lancaster, and I'm a vampire." That felt like safe info to give up.

"How old are you?"

Behind her back, she could feel her claws extend a bit more. "Haven't you heard? You're not supposed to ask a woman her age. That's just rude. Extremely poor manners."

The faintest smile curved his lips. "Are you a new vamp or have you been around for a while?"

"I'm fresh." She cleared her throat. "I mean new." Crap, did he know about the slang term for newly made vamps? Freshblood? Surely he did, since the guy *was* the Para Unit. She just had to act weak and timid a bit more and he'd buy her ruse, she was sure of it.

"Really." He leaned forward and his hand slid inside his coat. He pulled out—a wooden stake. Oh, crap. Things were definitely about to get real in there. "I would have pegged you for an older vampire."

Her gaze locked on the stake as Eric twirled it between his fingers. "What are you doing with that?" A stake to the heart would freeze a vampire. Totally incapacitate her. She wouldn't die, not unless he followed up the stake attack by cutting off her head. But—

He threw the stake at her. It flashed, whirling end over end in a deadly arc that was directed straight at her chest.

She grabbed that stake right out of the air before it could land in her heart. Then she flew across the room. *Okay,* she didn't technically fly, but she moved so fast that she knew it would look like a big blur to him, and in a flash, Ella had that stake shoved at his throat. "Do you enjoy torturing vampires?" Ella snarled at him.

He didn't fight her. Her body was sprawled on top of his as he continued to lounge on her couch. She could feel his strength, but he wasn't using it against her.

No, he'd just tried to stake me, that's all. Bastard.

"You're not Freshblood," he said softly. He almost sounded pleased, satisfied, as if she'd passed some kind of test for him.

"This is what's going to happen," Ella said, fighting to keep her voice steady. "That jerk you've got behind the glass? The one watching us now—videoing our interaction or whatever the hell it is that he's supposed to be doing—that guy is going to open the cell door. He's going to clear a path so that I can get out of this prison. And *you're* going to let me walk away. I'll vanish, and we never have to see each other again."

His gaze held hers. "And why would that happen?"

She pressed the sharp end of that stake deeper against his throat. "Because if you don't order him to do as I've said, I will shove this stake into your throat. Do you think you'll stay alive long enough for help to get to you?" Ella pretended to consider the matter. "I don't think so. I don't—"

"You don't bluff that well."

She certainly did!

"You're strong, your reflexes are off the charts, and you move with the speed of a vamp who has been around a very long time."

Mistake three, mistake four, mistake – screw it! I won't count them now.

"Yes, you are many things, Ella..."

A shiver slid over her. There was something about the way he said her name. A deep caress in his voice that unnerved her.

"But I don't think you are stupid."

She growled, "That's good to know."

"Because killing me? That would be a dumb move. If you murdered the head of the Para Unit, what do you think would happen to you?"

Nothing good.

"How about I tell you what would happen?" Eric murmured. "You'd lose this plush cell and be on the next boat to Purgatory. The guards would throw you in a cage and you'd stay there for the rest of your very, very long life. If the werewolves there didn't kill you—I've heard some of them are very attracted to vampire females—then I'm sure there would be plenty of other hell for you to enjoy."

The stake was still at his throat. Her legs were on either side of his hips as she straddled him on the couch. She stared into his eyes, and, for a moment, she truly hated him.

Ella snapped the stake in her hand and tossed the pieces of wood aside.

He nodded. "See, I said you weren't good at bluffing. I knew you weren't going to kill me."

"And how'd you know that? Trust me, buddy, I'm plenty tempted right now."

His hands rose and curled around her hips. For the first time, her position took on a very sexual tone. A tone that she didn't want. "Let me go."

"You're the one who came after me."

"You're the one who tried to *stake* me first!"

His smile stretched a bit. He had an oddly disarming smile. Good thing she wasn't the type to be disarmed.

"You lied to me, so I just tested that lie," Eric explained.

"With a stake?" Ella gritted out.

"It wouldn't have killed you."

Her chest seemed to burn. "No, but it would have hurt. If it had hit my heart, it would have paralyzed me."

His smile dimmed.

"But I guess my pain is acceptable for you."

Eric glanced away from her. "Actually, it's not. I don't…like that idea."

She laughed. "You know what, Eric? You're not very good at lying." Her hands pushed against his chest. That push should have been enough to have her easily breaking free from him.

If he'd just been human, she *would* have been free.

But her push didn't make him move. He tightened his hold on her hips, and Ella was too aware of his strength.

Lowering her voice, she said, "You're the man who chains up the monsters. Do the men and women who work for you even realize that *you're* a monster, too?"

A muscle flexed in his jaw.

She brought her mouth close to his right ear and Ella whispered, "I guess I'm not the only one with secrets, am I?"

He stiffened beneath her.

Then, in the next instant, Eric had put Ella on her feet and he'd jumped up to her side. "We're done for the day," he snapped. The guy marched for the door.

Ella blinked and stared after him. *Done?* No, done meant he'd leave her and she'd be trapped alone in her cell again. "Stop!"

He didn't stop.

So she just sped right past him. Before he could reach the door, Ella was in his path. They nearly collided, but he pulled back at the last moment.

"Don't lock me in again," Ella said. She hated the pleading note in her voice. "I've been a prisoner too long. Your prisoner. *His* prisoner. I want to be free. That's all I want."

Emotion flashed in his gaze—and she could feel the swirl of those emotions in the air around her. Desire, rage…such a dangerous combination.

And…pity?

Ella straightened her spine. "I haven't hurt anyone." Despite that little show with the stake. She'd restrained herself. "Let me go."

"I'm sorry." His gaze swept over her face. "I can't."

Then he walked around her.

Ella didn't move.

She heard his fist pound into the door. Obviously, that was a signal for the guards to let him out because the clang of the bolt in that lock rang a few seconds later. She looked over her shoulder and saw the door open. And Eric strode out.

Her body turned toward the door. Ella took a tentative step toward it.

The guard slammed the door shut.

Clang. The heavy lock slid back into place.

At that moment, something inside of Ella seemed to splinter—or maybe *she* splintered. Into a thousand pieces.

***

His hands were shaking.

Eric Pate took a deep breath and tried to yank his control back into place. He never lost his control. *Never.*

"Uh, boss?"

His hands clenched into fists.

"Are you sure we're doing the right thing with her?" Connor Marrok asked as he moved to Eric's side. Both men were staring through the observation glass, watching Ella.

She stood near the locked door. Her shoulders were slumped. Her long, dark hair fell forward, concealing her face.

"I don't like locking up victims," Connor continued, his voice roughening. "I saw her in that hellhole. That bastard Keegan had her chained up. He'd nearly starved her…"

Eric made a mental note to remove Connor from Ella's rotation. The other man felt too much sympathy for her.

Right, like I don't?

When he'd been in that room with her, when she'd stared up at him with tears glinting in her gorgeous eyes, his chest had begun to burn.

When she'd asked not to be locked in again, he'd almost set her free right then. Almost offered her anything, *everything* to just not look at him that way.

As if he were a monster.

"We aren't hurting her," Eric said and his voice was gruff to his own ears. "We're helping her to heal. She needed to be monitored after what she endured with Keegan." That sick, twisted bastard of a werewolf. A werewolf who had actually turned out to be Connor's long lost brother. *Talk about a twisted family tree.*

"We have monitored her," Connor said. "You've tested her plenty. You've given her your drugged blood. Until today, she didn't fight anyone." He turned his head and glanced at Eric, his golden eyes glinting. "Until you went at her with a stake..."

Eric locked his jaw even as he felt shame burn through him. *I had to do my job. I don't like my damn job, but I had to test her. It was necessary.* "I knew she wasn't a Freshblood. I knew she'd catch that stake."

"What if you'd been wrong?" Connor asked, not pulling any punches. "What if the great Eric Pate had actually made a mistake? But then, I guess it wouldn't be the first time you staked a vamp. If the stories are true, you even staked your sister once."

Eric swallowed. That particular story *was* true. But he'd only staked his step-sister, Holly, in order to protect her. She'd been heading out toward certain death. His job—always—was to protect his sister.

"You think I get to make the easy choices?" Eric asked, his voice low. Ella had known she was being watched, so he wondered just how much of their conversation she might be overhearing. "Nothing I do is easy." He exhaled on a long sigh. "But Holly had run her tests on...on Ella." A strangely disarming name. "Some interesting anomalies appeared, and I knew she wasn't some weak, new vamp that Keegan had captured."

Connor's brows shot up. "Just what kind of anomalies are you talking about?"

"The kind that make me nervous. The kind that even Holly can't understand—and she's the best expert on paranormal genetics that we've got." He glanced back through the observation window. "Ella's not *just* a vampire. At least, according to Holly, she isn't."

He could feel the tension rocking up as Connor leaned closer to the one-way mirror. The guy was now studying Ella with new suspicion. "You think she's like me?"

"A vamp and werewolf mix? A cross-over?" A deadly combination. "I sure as hell hope not." But there were other things to fear in the world, too. "For a while, I thought we were just hunting vamps and wolves. Now…because of her…I'm wondering if other things could be out there, too."

"Other…*things?*" Connor's voice roughened. "She's a woman, first and foremost. She's not a damn thing, and you have to stop thinking like that."

Connor didn't understand. He probably never would. Eric couldn't let his control down. He couldn't risk empathizing too much with his prisoners. If he did—

Her head snapped up. Her gaze—so wide and deep and filled with pain and fury—locked on his. No hesitation. She just zeroed right in on him, as if the mirror weren't even between them.

"Trust me," he heard himself murmur. "I am highly aware that she's a woman."

A woman who was now striding straight toward him.

"Ah, correction," Connor said, "that is one very *pissed* woman."

Her cheeks burned red. Her delicate jaw locked and when she lifted her hands, Eric could see the small claws that had grown from her fingertips.

"Uh, Eric…"

She stopped on the other side of the glass, standing directly in front of Eric. Her shoulders shuddered with every gasping breath that she took.

"I *won't* be a prisoner again." Ella's voice was loud and clear. Her eyes glittered. "You can't keep me here. You *won't!*" Then she lifted her hands, balled them into fists, and started smashing the glass.

She'll hurt herself. She –

"It's reinforced, right?" Connor said, his voice flat.

It was. "She has to stop," Eric said. "She'll just hurt her hands. All of the cells here are paranormal proof, and even if she hadn't been taking the drugged blood – "

The glass started to break beneath her fists.

Every muscle in Eric's body locked down. "That's not possible."

"Yeah, it is!" Now Connor was letting his own claws out. "Guess we're seeing those anomalies you mentioned." His clawed hand reached for the red button that would sound the alarm.

Ella bared her fangs at Eric. Fangs that weren't quite as long as a normal vamp's. More delicate. Then she drove her fist into the glass and it shattered, falling down around them.

Connor swore and slammed down the alarm.

But Eric didn't move. The broken glass reigned down around him and he stared into Ella's blazing gaze. Nothing separated them now. Nothing at all.

He probably shouldn't have noticed how incredibly gorgeous she was in that moment. But he did. He'd been drawn to her from the first instant. Such a very, very dangerous thing.

For them both.

"I won't be a prisoner!" Ella yelled. "Not anymore."

Then she leapt right at him.

CHAPTER TWO

An alarm was shrieking, making her head pound, and blood dripped from her hands as Ella shot through that now destroyed observation window and went straight for Eric.

He was the one she needed. He was the one who was trying to keep her captive. He was the one who *would* free her.

She launched straight at him, her fury nearly choking her. Fury and pain and fear. The emotions raged in her, a terrible fire that couldn't be quenched. And that fury wasn't just directed at Eric…

No, it went back longer—back to that bastard Keegan who'd kept her chained in his basement. He'd starved her. Taken her blood. Made her drink from him.

And he broke something in me.

She could tell. She was damaged and she wanted her old life back. *I'll take it back!*

Her body collided with Eric's and they fell to the stone floor. He was beneath her, so he took the full force of the impact. That was the least of what he deserved. She shoved upward and her nails went for his throat.

Her wrist—both of her wrists—were instantly trapped in a rock hard grip. Not Eric's grip—the guard's.

"Sorry," a gravelly male voice rumbled, coming from her left. "As tempting as it is, I can't let you kill the guy."

Eric stared up at her. His pupils had expanded, the black dominating now in his eyes. "She wasn't going to kill me, Connor."

The alarm was still ringing, nearly shattering her mind. It was so terribly loud.

She jerked against the hold on her wrists, trying to break free with a mighty heave—but the guy held her tight.

"Can't do that," the one called Connor said, "you'll just go for his throat again."

Her head whipped toward him. Through her fury and fear, she…recognized him. His eyes were pure gold as they held hers. There was no fury in his gaze. No hate. Just stoic determination. His hair was a little too long, dark, and his face was cut in hard, almost rough lines.

That face—she could never forget it. "You saved me." She stopped fighting him because she owed this man. Yes, she thought she could break free of his grip, but he'd be…damaged…in that battle. "You were the one who got me out of that basement." The fire had been raging around her, and she'd been trapped.

Then this man—this agent—had appeared. He'd broken the manacles that locked around her and she'd rushed from the house. Only she hadn't gone far until she'd found herself tumbling straight into Eric's arms.

Before he could respond, a door burst open—a door that led to the observation room that they were in. A team of agents—all dressed so stereotypically in black—stormed inside. They were all armed and their guns pointed straight at Ella.

She was still crouched over Eric. He wasn't moving at all. And Connor had her wrists in his powerful grip.

Her heartbeat thundered in her ears. For a moment, that frantic sound was so loud that it nearly drowned out the terrible screech of the alarm.

"Stand down," Eric said, his voice strong with command. "And someone, please, shut off that fucking alarm."

The agents in black lowered their guns.

The alarm stopped a moment later.

"If I let go of your hands," Connor said, "you can't go for his throat."

Ella gave a grim nod. She knew if she so much as twitched, the agents would probably open fire on her. Since she didn't know what sort of bullets were in their guns, she didn't want to take any additional risks.

Connor let go of her hands. She kept them in the air, wanting to show the other agents that she wasn't a threat. At least, not at that moment, she wasn't.

"Orders, sir?" One of the men in black barked. She didn't look at him, but she did turn her gaze back to Eric.

He was watching her. She wondered if he'd been staring at her the whole time.

A chill slid over her. *He's always watching me.*

"My orders are to back out of this room. Your fast response is certainly appreciated, but I have things under control."

There was a quick cough, and then the guy asked, "You sure about that, sir?"

Eric smiled up at Ella. It was a rather chilling smile. "I'm dead certain, Lawrence. Now get the hell out."

"Sir!"

Footsteps thudded in a quick retreat. She still had her hands up—until the last agent shut the door behind him.

"I'm not complaining," Eric mused, "I rather like the view I currently have, but if you prefer to stand while we talk—"

She shot to her feet. Glared at him.

He rose slowly. "I thought as much. Pity." He glanced down at her hands, and all traces of humor left his face. He grabbed her wrists and pulled her toward him. "You're bleeding."

She looked down. Blood coated her knuckles and she might have broken some fingers.

"I'll heal." She cleared her throat, then pointedly said, "I'd heal better without drugged blood but—"

He was hauling her toward the door. "Call for Holly," he threw the order at Connor. "Get her to meet us in exam room two."

Holly. The name chilled Ella. She knew Holly was the pretty doctor who'd done all of the experiments on her after Ella had been brought to the facility. Holly had been incredibly kind, incredibly professional—and Ella really wanted to *never* see the other woman again.

But I don't have a choice. Not if my plan is going to work.

"No." She dug in her heals. After all, she had to play this part. "The wounds will be gone soon. I'll be okay."

"Your hands are broken," he rasped. "Your blood..." He was lightly holding her hands now. Her blood had dripped onto him. "I didn't mean—you need medical treatment."

That was the least of what she needed.

But...*Non-drugged blood will help me. In fact, it's exactly what I need.*

A few moments later, Ella found herself seated on an examining table. Holly was in front of her. The woman's thick hair had been pulled back into a ponytail at the nape of her neck, and her dark gaze was serious as she carefully patched Ella's hands.

Eric watched every movement from his position not two feet away. Every time that Ella so much as hissed in pain—mild pain, because she'd had so much worse in her life—Eric swore. What was up with that? The guy was acting as if he actually cared.

"You were the one throwing a stake at me not long ago," she groused at him.

Holly gave a little jerk.

"Now you're mad because I'm bleeding a bit?" Ella shook her head. "You're an odd man, Eric Pate."

"The stake was never going to touch you," he muttered. "We both know that. *You shouldn't have been hurt.*"

She rolled her eyes. "Sorry. Didn't get that memo. Maybe you should start sending the memos out to prisoners, too, and not just your guards."

He growled at her.

It was a rough, animalistic sound.

Deep inside, a part of her…liked it.

That wasn't good. She didn't need to like anything about her jailer.

"You're a vampire," Holly said softly as she took a step back, finally seeming to finish her work. Ella hadn't really been paying much attention to what the woman was doing to her hands. "So your bones should mend soon—"

"Yeah, they'd mend faster if I was given some non-drugged blood." That wasn't a subtle hint. She didn't feel subtle. Her gaze slid to Eric. "So why don't you give me the good stuff? I mean, if you really don't want me in pain."

He gave a grim nod.

Wait, what? He was going to give it to her? *Yes!*

"Give her the blood."

Ella tried to hide her surprise. She'd figured that request was a serious long shot, but since it had worked, maybe she'd try pushing a bit more... "It would be ever better," Ella said, staring into Eric's gaze, "if I could take from a live source."

Holly hurriedly backed away. Ella figured the doctor was going for some bagged blood. *Hurry up with that, please.*

But when Holly retreated, Eric stepped forward. He leaned in close, putting his hands on either side of her body, caging her on that exam table. "Are you asking for a bite?"

"Yes."

He smiled at her. A dangerous but tempting smile. "I know what happens with a vampire's bite. Are you trying to get inside my head? Control me?"

Absolutely. That was the benefit of biting prey. Mind control. And as soon as she could control him, then she'd be home free.

"Holly," Eric called out, but he kept his gaze on Ella. "I'll take care of Ella. You don't have to worry about the bagged blood."

"*Eric.*" Okay, that was absolute horror in the other woman's voice. "You can't!"

He shrugged and undid the button on the cuff of his sleeve. "Sure I can. I'm the director. I can do anything."

This wasn't happening. Was it?

Still staring at her, Eric slowly rolled up his sleeve, revealing a wide, thick wrist. Tanned skin.

He turned his wrist toward her, and Ella could see the faint tracing of his veins. Hunger hit her, sharp and hard. She hadn't tasted from prey directly since—

She immediately shut down that thought.

Desperate times call for desperate measures.

"You know what a vampire's bite can do," Holly said, her voice sharp. "*You know, Eric.*"

Ella couldn't take her eyes off his exposed skin. Her teeth had sharpened, her fangs more than ready to taste him.

"I know exactly what I'm doing," Eric responded. He didn't even sound mildly concerned. His mistake. It was good that he was the one making mistakes now and not her.

"Thanks for checking her out, Holly. You can leave us alone now."

Silence.

Then…the pad of Holly's footsteps as she headed for the door. The clang as that door closed seemed incredibly loud.

Ella became aware that her breath was coming far too fast. She dragged her gaze off his wrist and back up to his face. His eyes glittered at her. "Is this some kind of trick?"

He shook his head. "I handled you wrong. My apologies."

Handled her?

"Containment was for your protection, though you may not believe that." He inclined his head toward her. "Now I must insist that you heal because I really don't like to see you in pain."

That was a new one. Her hand reached for his. She lifted his wrist toward her mouth. Her fangs were fully extended—not as long as a normal vamp's, but still more than sharp enough to get the job done. Staring into his eyes, she brought her mouth to his wrist.

His lips parted. His nostrils flared.

A vampire's bite could be painful. Humiliating. It could bring agony to the vamp's prey.

Or it could bring pleasure.

Her teeth sank into him. Eric hissed out a sharp breath and his blood flowed over her tongue. Rich and warm and heady. The rush that his blood gave her was immediate. Far too powerful. Her head spun and she felt dizzy. Wanting more. Needing more.

Wanting to take…*all.*

"Ella…" He whispered her name, desire roughening his voice.

I won't be a monster. No matter what the stories say. I won't.

Her tongue licked over his skin and she forced herself to pull back. His blood was different, but, then, she'd known he wasn't human. She just hadn't expected to feel that burst of raw power rushing through her whole body.

It felt as if she'd been guzzling champagne. And some serious, hard core energy drinks.

She needed more.

"Thank you," Ella whispered.

A muscle jerked in his jaw. "Trust me, the pleasure was all mine." His cheeks had flushed and his voice was a sexy rumble.

He didn't back away from her. She found that she couldn't move at all. "What are you?" Ella asked him. Then she licked her lips, still savoring his taste. She'd been walking the earth for a long time, but she'd never hungered for more the way she did with him.

His lips curled. "I could ask you the same thing."

"Vampire," she threw back at him. That was an easy enough—and the most obvious—response for her.

"And what else?" He wanted to know.

That part, she wouldn't tell.

Her hand lifted. Her bones were already snapping back into place.

Eric swore. "Damn, that was—"

"Fast. You'd be amazed at what fresh blood can do for me." The healing was just the start. She was about to bust out of that place and never look back.

There was a reason that sick twisted freak Keegan had kept her starved in that basement. He'd known that if he gave her any fresh blood, he'd never be able to control her. She was too strong.

Eric was about to see that strength.

It had been a risky plan. Acting all crazy and slamming her fists into the glass. She'd had to be careful. And she'd had to wager that Eric wouldn't let her just bleed all over him. But…but there had been something between them in her cell.

She'd seen a softening in his gaze when he looked at her. Eric should have known better. You could never soften when an enemy was near.

Unfortunately, it would seem they were meant to be enemies. He was one side. The *good* side. And she—

Wasn't.

So she'd broken her hands. Cut herself deeply on the glass and waited for Eric to play knight in shining armor. Men with hero complexes were so incredibly predictable, even when they tried to play the role of the bad boy. She could see right through them.

She'd just needed fresh blood to get stronger. She'd never imagined the guy would actually be crazy enough to offer himself up as her prey. "You should have listened to the doctor," Ella told him a bit sadly.

"She's my sister."

"What?"

"Step-sister…my family. So I'll take it pretty personally if anything ever happens to her."

She got the message. He was warning her not to hurt the doc. "I can understand family." For a moment, grief pulled at her, but she shoved the emotion back. Now wasn't the time to let that particular ghost loose. "Your sister was right though, letting a vampire have your blood is a terrible mistake."

"Is it?"

She stared into his eyes. "I want you to back away from me."

Jaw clenching, he did.

That dizziness she felt got a little worse. His blood had given her a serious head rush. She'd gone way too long without the good stuff. And his blood was very, very good.

Ella jumped off that exam table. For an instant, her knees wobbled.

He reached for her.

"Don't!" Ella snapped.

He froze.

She straightened. "I'm fine." More than fine now. He was obeying her every command. That was the way of it. When a vampire took from prey, the vamp could control that victim. Mind control wasn't normally her favorite tool of choice. It made her feel…bad. But right then, she didn't care how morally ambiguous it was.

She'd be getting out of that place. And Eric would be her escort so no other guards or agents or whatever the hell they were tried to stop her. "You're going to escort me to the exit. You're going to make sure no one tries to put me in a cell again."

He exhaled. "You aren't going back to containment."

"Damn right, I'm not." She smiled at him. "Take me out of here."

His hand curled around her waist. The move was unexpected, but she didn't stop him. Ella figured they might look more natural—definitely chummier—this way. They left the med area.

Two guards and Holly started to approach them as they swept into the hallway, but Eric waved them back.

Yes! Satisfaction poured through Ella. This was awesome. Absolutely fantastic.

Their steps were in sync as they headed down a long corridor. Her heart beat faster. Freedom was so close. So incredibly close.

They passed more of those rather intimidating men in their black uniforms. Their guns were way too close for comfort.

"Tell them to stand down," Ella said immediately.

She thought Eric sighed, but then he said, "Stand down."

Her body relaxed against his. A few more minutes and—yes! She thought they were in front of the exit door. He waved the guards away there, too. But before Ella could grab that door and race away, Eric was in her path.

"There's something you should know."

She didn't really want to know anything else. "Just get out of my way…and…and forget you ever so much as saw me." She focused hard on him while she gave that final command.

But he didn't get out of her way. Instead, he gave a sad shake of his head as he said, "I don't think it's easy to forget a woman like you."

Something was wrong. "You aren't supposed to say that."

He shrugged.

"Get. Out. Of. My. Way."

Eric crossed his arms over his broad chest and just stared back at her. "There are a few things you need to be aware of, Ella."

"You're not under my control." She barely breathed those words as shock sent icy tendrils over her skin.

"What? Oh, no. I'm not. Sorry. Did you think I was?"

The jerk! Yes, she'd thought—

"I'm not exactly susceptible to a vampire bite, at least not the control part." For an instant, desire glinted in his eyes. "I wasn't quite expecting it to feel so good though."

What the hell? He was talking as if her bite had been some kind of science experiment!

Eric leaned in closer. "You were right before. When you said I wasn't human. Nice of you to notice." His voice carried only to her. "Most others don't."

The door was so close. Freedom was steps away.

"I want to make a deal with you," Eric said.

"No, you just want to play games with me. Screw with my head." She could actually smell the night. It was calling to her. Taunting her now.

"You were in containment for your protection, but I realize now, I should have…handled you differently."

And they were back to the 'handling' bit. "Your social skills need so much work it isn't even funny."

He blinked.

Her hands curled into fists. Maybe the blood bond between them didn't give her control because of *whatever* the guy was. But his blood *had* given her some rather desperately needed strength. "I don't want to hurt you." That was actually true. If she'd wanted to hurt him, she would have shoved that stake into his throat. Instead, she'd held back. "But I am getting out of this place. No more tests. No more poking and prodding. No more watching me all the time. I'm leaving." Her shoulders straightened. "So get out of my way before you see my really dark side."

One brow shot up. "The deal will be open for twenty-four hours."

Had she not just told him to move?

"We didn't find a body." After that flat announcement, Eric finally stepped aside.

She took a fast lunging step forward. Her hands touched that door.

And—

Ella glanced back at him. "Body?"

"Um. Remember that hellish place Keegan kept you in?"

Her eyes turned to slits.

"Right, of course you do. Well, it burned to the ground. And maybe Keegan burned with it."

Escape had been her only goal one moment before. Now she was rooted to the spot.

"His remains weren't found," Eric said grimly.

"Maybe the fire was too hot. Keegan—he was part wolf, part vampire." *Because the bastard made me change him.* "Vampires burn fast. Everyone knows that." Well, everyone who realized vampires actually existed knew that.

"I haven't seen one of his…type die before," Eric allowed. "So maybe you're right. But what I do know is that when alpha werewolves actually survive a transition and become both beast and vamp, they seem to develop all of the strengths of each paranormal, and none of the weaknesses."

She pushed open the door. The night air whispered over her skin. She had absolutely no idea where this building was located, and she didn't care. Ella planned on just running until she was far, far away. Vamp speed would come in handy for her.

"If he is alive, aren't you afraid he'll come after you?" Eric asked.

Ah, so that was what his deal was about. He thought to offer her protection. In exchange for what? She glanced over her shoulder, giving him a cold smile. "I'm not the one who needs to be afraid. He won't catch me off-guard again. If Keegan is still alive, then he's the one who needs to fear *me.*" Because she would make him pay for all that he'd done to her.

"He controlled at least one pack. There could be more. You have to watch—"

"Good-bye, Eric Pate. I hope our paths never cross again."

Then she ran into the night. Faster, faster, faster…

Freedom.

It tasted even better than his blood.

***

She seemed to vanish in a blink. One moment, she was there, staring at him with her unforgettable gaze, seeming to see right into him, and the next…

Ella was gone.

Eric figured it would have been an easy enough matter for her to clear the tall, eight foot wall that surrounded the facility. She'd probably been able to do it in one bound.

Fast. So very fast.

"I don't like this plan, Eric."

He rolled back his shoulders when he heard Holly's voice. For most of their lives, Holly had pretty much been his moral compass. Mostly because his own sense of right and wrong could be skewed the majority of the time.

She was his sister, not by blood, but that hardly mattered to him. Their parents had married long ago, and she was the only family he had.

One brutal night, a vampire had tried to take Holly from him. He'd held her as she bled out on the street. And he'd seen what a real monster was.

It was me.

She'd survived that attack. She'd become a vampire, and now she worked with him at the Para Unit. After all, who better to patch up the monsters they brought in than a doctor who understood them so fully?

He sighed and said, "Did you slip the tracking chip beneath her skin?"

It had been a risky move. He'd planned to insert that chip before he released Ella, but he'd just been trying to figure out *how* to implant it without arousing her suspicion. Another trip to the med unit for more testing with Holly would have been met with resistance, so he'd been trying to bide his time.

Then an opportunity had presented itself so perfectly.

"You know," Holly mused, "when you first burst into the med unit, I actually bought that you were worried about her."

He was still staring into the night. It was strange, but he could have sworn Ella's scent lingered in the air. It was a nice scent. Sweet. "Lilacs."

"What?"

He cleared his throat. "I'm glad you understood what needed to be done." Holly had caught his eye when he'd burst in with Ella, and he'd given her the barest of nods. It had been an easy enough matter for Holly to slip that incredibly tiny device into one of Ella's open wounds, and then when he'd given her his blood, the wounds had just closed up right around it.

"Why can't you let her go? Don't you think she's been through enough?"

The night waited on him. How far away was she now? "The problem is that I have no idea what she's been through. She didn't talk to anyone I sent to her." At first, he'd mistakenly thought that Ella would only be too happy to share. After all, his team had freed her. She would be grateful, right?

Not. She'd refused to speak. Refused to cooperate at all. And a woman—a vampire who did that—*she has to be hiding something.*

There was a beat of silence behind him. Silence from his sister was never a good sign. Slowly, he glanced her way.

When their gazes connected, Holly said, "You're wrong."

She never believed in sugar coating with him. One of the many reasons why he loved her. And he'd die to protect her.

"She did talk to someone. After days of silence, you walked in and she immediately told you her name."

Yes, she had. Just how had Holly picked up that tidbit? "You've been with Connor, haven't you?" It figured the guy would share with Holly. Connor's brother, Duncan, was married to her.

Eric hadn't been thrilled about that alliance, not initially. But then he'd seen that Duncan was willing to go to hell and back for Holly. That had changed plenty for him.

"She talked to you," Holly continued. "I think that means something."

He wasn't sure what it meant. But he did know one thing. Being too close to Ella Lancaster was dangerous. She stirred urges in him, dark desires, that were better left alone. Control was important for him—and with good reason.

When his control splintered, people had a tendency to die.

"Why do you have to track her? Why—"

"Because I really do believe that Keegan James escaped that fire." Though he hadn't told anyone else that news.

Her dark eyes widened. "And you think he'll go after her?"

Eric laughed at that question. He had spent many, many hours watching Ella. Trying to see past her mask and learn her secrets. "No, I think she'll go after him."

And payback would be a real bitch for the werewolf who'd tried to break the beautiful vampiress.

CHAPTER THREE

Forty-eight hours later, Ella was ready for her vengeance. She'd showered. She'd slept. She'd gotten fresh clothes and more fresh blood. The fresh blood had come courtesy of some flirtatious young men. Frat boys could be so accommodating. Give them a little smile, and they'd blindly follow a strange woman into the nearest dark alley. They really better learn to watch themselves with that move.

The next vamp might not leave them alive.

She was in Washington, the state, not the district. She'd stayed away from the city, because she knew that werewolves didn't like the cities so much. They felt too contained in them. The cities made their beasts all antsy—poor pitiful things.

So she'd gone toward the woods. Caught their scent.

Now she was ready for some vengeance.

Ella stared at the building in front of her. From the outside, it hardly looked impressive. A wooden structure. Short. Squat. Music blared from inside, and an assortment of vehicles filled the lot.

Humans were in there. Blind humans who totally didn't understand the danger they faced.

And werewolves. At least four, judging by the scents she was picking up in the air. One of those scents was terribly familiar to her.

When she'd been taken, Ella had sworn never to forget the wolves who'd swarmed her.

And I just found one of that pack.

She sauntered toward the building, taking her time. She'd…acquired…a short mini skirt, and the cool air felt good as it blew over her legs. She was wearing boots with that skirt, what she thought were perfect, ass-kicking boots. And a black top completed her outfit—maybe that top showed off a lot of flesh. When the lure looked pretty enough, the fools always rushed in.

Frat boys. Werewolves.

They could all be the same.

She headed inside and paused just a few feet from the doorway. The interior was dim, but Ella could see perfectly. Her nose twitched the faintest bit, and then her head turned to the right. The four werewolves were playing pool at the back table. Acting as if they didn't have a care in the world.

She was about to make them care. About so many things.

Ella pushed back her shoulders. She straightened her spine, and then she closed in on her prey.

***

"She dragged us nearly to the Canadian border," Connor grumbled from beside Eric. They'd parked their SUV well away from Ella—and the bar she'd just entered. "Couldn't the woman have traveled a little more slowly? I mean, hell, it's like she's some kind of missile, locked and loaded."

Eric's fingers were poised over his laptop keyboard. "I think she is."

Connor turned toward him. "You really believe that bastard Keegan is alive?"

Ah, there was a whole lot of rage in Connor's voice. He needed to tread lightly here. "Careful, buddy, your beast is showing."

Connor growled.

"Still showing," Eric pointed out.

"Sorry. We can't all have ice in our veins like you do."

Was that what flowed through him? Not quite. "I told you, there is a possibility that he survived."

"I want him dead." Hard. Brutal. And, considering that Keegan had attacked the woman that Connor mated with—well, his rage was certainly understandable.

"We're not supposed to be executioners," Eric said carefully. "We're federal agents. Our job is to apprehend the criminals."

Connor's laughter was cold. "You think I don't get it? Hell, man, I'm understanding you better and better each day. You want him dead just as much as I do. I saw the way you looked at that little vampiress. You hate what that jerk did to her. And *that's* why you haven't already gone in there, guns blazing. You think she's killing him right now, and you're trying to give her the time she needs to get her vengeance." His fingers tapped along the steering wheel. "That's why I haven't gone in yet, too," Connor muttered. "Figure she deserves her payback, even more than I do."

Eric clenched his back teeth. "*If* Keegan isn't in there, and I go storming in…then she's going to realize we've been tracking her. I'm waiting out here just to see what happens next." And he was seriously wondering why he'd chosen to bring Connor on this mission.

Because he's helluva strong. And I might need some strong back-up.

"Right," Connor muttered. "Just keep telling yourself that. But I know you're hot for the vampiress…"

Helluva strong and helluva annoying.

***

She took her time closing in on that pool table, but the men tensed even before they saw her.

She'd expected that. For werewolves…a female vampire's scent could be particularly sweet. And her scent would be sweet enough to tempt them.

"Fuck," one growled. "Sex…and honey."

Yes, that was what she'd heard female vampires smelled like to werewolves. Now she understood why.

Only female vampires could transform an alpha werewolf—and make him into a truly unstoppable beast. The scent of a female was designed to lure in that alpha, and to seal both of their fates.

"Hello, boys," Ella called. The accent she'd once had was long gone now. She'd lived too long to keep any one accent. "Mind if I join this little game?"

They turned toward her as one. She could see the beast in their gazes.

She smiled, but didn't flash fang, not yet. Instead, she sauntered forward and took the pool cue from the tall, dark-haired werewolf to the right. The one with deep gray eyes and a slashing scar that ran down his cheek.

I remember you, jerkoff. Do you remember me? She liked to think of herself as pretty unforgettable.

"Y-you're a dead woman," the scarred werewolf said.

Ella sighed. "That is so insulting, and you *know* we're undead."

One of the other werewolves ran toward her. She just shoved the pool stick into his shoulder and thrust him back. His howl filled the bar.

Silence.

The really uncomfortable kind.

The werewolf's howl had attracted every eye in the place.

Ella glanced around. "This is probably a good time for most of you to leave." Rule number one in the paranormal world—*don't attract the attention of humans.* A good vamp fed on humans in secret. A good vamp didn't attack in a crowded bar. A good vamp didn't—

Screw it. She was too tired of being good. Being good had gotten her captured and starved.

No one moved. Humans just didn't obey instructions as well as they should.

The werewolf she'd just—um, pool cued—was rising and snarling and—shifting. Well, well, wasn't he the one who wasn't playing by the special paranormal rules, either?

Two others from that little pack jumped at her. She broke one guy's nose with a flick of her hand. She sent the other hurtling onto the pool table half a second later.

The shifting wolf was snarling and his bones were popping and the humans were screaming.

They were also *finally* fleeing. Good for them.

But the werewolf with a scar hadn't moved. He was staring at her with a sick smile on his face. "I remember you," he said.

"And I remember you." She wouldn't let the fury overwhelm her. "Tell me…do you still enjoy drugging vampires and then bleeding them out to the point where they are near death? Do you feel *good* when you do that?" She stepped toward him. "Strong? Like one real hell of a beast?"

He laughed at her, and he was the one to flash fang. Long, deadly fangs. His hand reached up, and black claws had sprung from his hands. Those claws lightly slid over her cheek. He didn't cut her. Good for him. Because if he'd so much as scratched her, she would have given him a new scar to enjoy.

"I *am* one hell of a beast," he murmured.

"I'm not drugged this time," Ella told him. "And if you want to see a beast…" She could feel the change starting to burn through her body. Her rage wouldn't be contained any more. Not while she was facing this bastard—and he dared to laugh at her. "Then get ready for what I'm about to show you."

***

A crowd ran out of that little bar as if they'd just seen a demon.

Or a vampire.

"Dammit," Eric said as he tossed aside the laptop and then shoved his car door open. He'd expected Ella to take her prey out back, the way she'd done with the college boys at the club the previous night. He hadn't expected her to flash fang in front of such a big group!

Cars were now racing out of the lot and one woman was screaming in the middle of that madness. "Monsters! *Monsters! Fucking monsters!*"

He ran up and touched the woman's shoulder. "Ma'am, you need to—"

She tried to punch him. He ducked the blow and brought up his ID. "Federal agent, ma'am. You need to calm the hell down."

She didn't. "*Fucking monsters!*"

"I think there may be a gas leak on the premises," he murmured as he tried to soothe her. "It's causing people to see things that aren't there."

Her mouth hung open.

"Are you experiencing dizziness? Maybe a headache?"

She put her hand to her temple. "I do feel light-headed."

That could be due to the fact that you smell like you swam in beer. "It's all right, ma'am. We just need to clear the scene. It's not safe for anyone to be inside right now."

Not safe for humans, anyway.

He glanced toward the bar's doors. No one else was running out. That meant it was time for him to go in. *Let's just see what hell Ella has managed to stir up.*

***

Ella could feel the cuts on her back as the skin near her shoulder blades burst open. It was a pain she hadn't allowed herself to feel in a very, very long time. Her body hunched forward as the change swept over her. Painful, consuming.

"*What the fuck...*" The scarred werewolf demanded, "*are you?*"

Ella smiled up at him. "I'm your death."

He backed away. Her fangs were out, her claws ready to go in for the kill. And behind her...she could feel the stretch of new muscle. New power. New—

The doors slammed open. "*Ella!*"

That roar was oddly familiar. For just a second, Ella glanced over her shoulder.

Eric stood in the doorway. Oh, how cute. He had a gun in his hand.

She didn't need guns.

Her shift was complete. She was whole again.

Her body began to lift, rising as she stretched her wings. Literally.

"Holy shit," the werewolf gasped.

She saw Eric's gaze go wild with total shock. "Ella?"

Her eyes narrowed on him, then she turned to the prey that mattered. The scarred wolf. Ella flew right at him. Her arms locked around him, and she lifted him up, holding him easily. Gunfire echoed behind her, followed by screams, but Ella didn't stop. She burst through the window with her prize, and then she flew straight out into the night.

***

He'd shot three werewolves. They were currently on the floor, groaning in agony because their bodies were full of silver. They weren't a threat to him, not anymore.

But Ella…

Eric ran to the broken window. She was gone. Long gone again. Only this time, she hadn't run away from him. She'd *fucking flown.*

Connor burst into the bar. "What the hell just happened?"

Eric swiped a hand over his face. "A problem I didn't anticipate."

"Did I just see that vampiress with *wings? Wings?*"

He had. Her wings had been big, beautiful, and a strange mix of gold and black as they shot straight from her back. They'd looked like silk as they'd fluttered around her.

Impossible.

"What kind of paranormal has wings?" Connor demanded.

"The kind that flies," Eric responded. He hadn't recognized that scarred werewolf, but for Ella to take him, then that meant the guy was important. The key to finding Keegan? *If* the bastard was still alive?

"Stay with them," Eric ordered as he waved his hand to the prone werewolves. One had been in the form of a beast when Eric shot him, but the guy had shifted back and was now sprawled naked amid a broken pile of beer bottles. "I'll send back-up to you. Take the wolves in and keep them contained until I can get answers."

He hurried to the door.

Connor grabbed his arm. "And just where are you going, boss?"

Eric glanced at the broken window. "She was really quite stunning, wasn't she?"

"Oh, shit, you are—"

"I'm finishing the mission. I'm following Ella, and I'm seeing just what she can lead me to."

Vengeance.

Or hell.
Eric figured it would be a toss-up.

CHAPTER FOUR

Her wings didn't normally come out. That part of her life had been nearly wiped away centuries before, and it took a whole lot of fury for her to shift these days.

But at that moment, she had plenty of rage pouring through her. So much so that Ella could barely *breathe* through her fury.

"Is Keegan alive?" Ella demanded as she held tightly to the werewolf.

He twisted, struggling in her arms. "Bitch, you ca—"

She dropped him. His scream seemed to shake the very earth. Ella counted. *One, two…*

Then she swung in and before *three* – before the big, bad werewolf would have gone all splat—she caught him. Then she shot straight up into the air again. "Let's try that once more. Is Keegan alive?'

"Yes! Fuck, yes! He survived!"

Her hold on him tightened. "Where is he?"

"Just…get me on the ground, and I'll tell you."

"I'll *drop* you to the ground if you don't tell me, right now."

"H-hiding out! He's burned, badly. He can't seem to heal from the wounds. Don't know why…maybe he was hurt too much. He's got a place, just over the border. He fled the US because he didn't want that damn Para Unit coming after him."

"He doesn't have to worry about them." She lowered them to the ground. "He has to worry about me."

The moonlight shone down on them. He had to be feeling the call of the beast, but he wasn't transforming. Curious now, her head tilted as she stared at him. "Who are you?"

"Reece."

The name meant nothing to her. "You're in his pack. You were there the night he took me."

"I-I was just following orders!"

Her hand lifted and traced his scar. "How'd you get this memento?"

He didn't answer.

She smiled. "Let me guess. You pissed off Keegan."

He was sweating. But not shifting. Interesting. Odd.

"What will happen when Keegan finds out that you told me exactly where he is?"

And then…Reece laughed.

She didn't like that laughter. It made her fury flare higher. *They laughed the night they drugged me. When they drained the blood from me.*

"We knew you'd come looking for us," Reece suddenly said. "Four in the bar? Just four? Come on, you know a pack is bigger than that."

Her gaze cut to the darkness of the trees.

"They followed you the minute you flew away with me. Keegan always suspected what you really were, and now we have proof."

Her hands fell away from him as she backed up, worried now that she'd missed a threat. Her rage had made her careless…

"I've heard stories about those wings. About just what they can do." His head tilted and he lifted his claws toward her. "Tell me…just how badly will it hurt when I cut them off you?"

"Come and try," Ella whispered. "You come and—"

He lunged.

She snarled.

More gunfire blasted.

Ella paused, her gaze on Reece. He was just inches away from her and—he was bleeding. She could smell his blood and the deeper, thicker scent of silver in the air. *Liquid silver?*

Reece fell to the ground, gasping.

Her attention snapped to the shooter. To the man who was striding slowly out of those woods.

To the guy who looked as if he didn't have a care in the world.

"What have you done?" Ella whispered.

"Don't worry, he's not dead," Eric said. "I didn't aim for the heart or the head. The silver will keep him down and the little…drug…that Holly added to the mix will keep him out until my men can transport him to containment."

Her wings fluttered behind her. Fury still rode her hard, so those wings weren't about to shift away. *Good. I'll need them to take me out of here.*

Because if she didn't move, fast, Eric's men would be arriving and transporting *her* to containment, too.

"Stay away from me."

"Keegan is alive. I heard the guy's words, Ella." He advanced slowly. Completely, *not* staying away. Someone couldn't follow directions well. "You need me."

"If you heard him…" Her gaze cut around them. "Then you should know…others are here."

"No, he was probably just bluffing, there's no sign of—"

Five fully shifted werewolves sprang from the trees. Ella screamed and immediately flew straight up into the air but—but there was a blast, as if someone had fired a gun—and a thick, heavy net circled her.

As soon as the net touched her skin, Ella knew she was in trouble. Her body began to sag as it reacted to the gold in that net. *Clever bastards.* Not heavy gold, just the faintest threads, but enough to do serious damage to her.

She screamed again, this time in pain.

"Ella!"

Through the netting, she saw Eric shooting at the wolves. He aimed with deadly accuracy and didn't so much as flinch when they rushed at him.

Bam.

One down.

Bam.

Another.

Ba—

The remaining wolves slammed into Eric and he went down in a swirl of growls and snarls as the beasts attacked him.

"No!" Ella yelled. "No, stop it! Let him go! Stop!" Fury pounded through her, and her wings stretched a bit more. The gold burned them, melting into her wings and she cried out in agony.

And then…

The werewolves who'd attacked Eric were tossed through the air. One hit the ground and gave a faint whimper.

Another—another slammed into a tree. He bounced back up quickly, and then he ran straight for Eric once more. Eric didn't have his gun any longer, and he grabbed at the wolf with both hands, holding tightly to the beast. They rolled on the ground, twisting and turning, and the wolf snapped at Eric with bared fangs. Ella was helpless, trapped in that golden net, feeling it burn her wings. The gold would forever mark them now, just as it had in the past when she'd been captured.

"Eric…" He was her only hope. If he didn't beat that wolf, then she'd be taken. So would her wings.

The wolf sank his teeth into Eric's shoulder. *"Eric!"* Ella screamed. A werewolf bite was fatal to a human, and if it didn't kill the prey—

Eric's not human. You know that. You know—

Eric's hand drove down toward his ankle. When his hand came back up, she caught the glint of metal. *Silver.* He swiped out with his blade. Blood splattered in an arc. And then he hit his prey again. Not swiping this time, but driving the knife straight at the snarling werewolf.

Then…silence.

Ella glanced around. The werewolves were down. Eric had taken them all. And now he was rising. Bleeding, but rising, and he was heading toward her.

She was crouched on the ground. That stupid net was all around her. Utterly helpless, she just waited to see what would happen next.

Containment. He'll take me back. He'll lock me up –

"The deal…" Eric muttered, sounding slightly out of breath. Slightly. After he'd just taken down a whole pack. "Is still…on the table…"

She blinked up at him. Ella felt tears on her cheeks. When had she started to cry?

"I…help you," Eric continued. "You…help me."

In that moment, she would have agreed to anything.

"Say it," Eric pushed. "Say –"

"Deal."

He ripped the net off her. She cried out in pain as the gold seemed to be ripped right from her wings. Then the shift pushed through her because the pain was too great. Her body heaved and twisted on the ground as the transformation swept over her. The back of her shirt tore even more, and the top fell away from her as she lay on the ground, crying in pain and hating so much…

What she was.

What had happened to her.

"Deal," Eric's voice was oddly soft. He reached down and wrapped his arms around her. He lifted her up and held her against his chest. "It's okay. I've got you."

She kept her lashes closed because she didn't want to see his expression. Not then. Pity was an emotion she'd always hated to the depths of her being. She was fine with others fearing her. Or hating her.

But pitying her?

Hell, no.

Then she heard the fast thud of footsteps. It sounded as if a dozen men were rushing their way. More of the pack? She hadn't caught their scent before and now—

"They're coming!" Ella said as her eyes flew open. Frantic, her gaze locked on Eric's.

There's no pity there. It was hard to say just what emotion filled his stare, but she knew with certainty, it wasn't pity.

"My men," Eric told her. "My back-up. They'll take care of the wolves." Then he turned, and still carrying her, he headed into the woods once more. "And I'll take care of you."

That was nice. Such sweet words. It was a pity they were a lie. He didn't want to take care of her. He wanted to use her. And because she'd made a deal with him—*does he know more about my kind than he's saying? She certainly thought so*—there would be no running away. They were bound now, until the deal had ended.

So she didn't fight his hold. Her body slumped against his. "I'll need blood again," she said. "And not the drugged crap, either." Just so they were clear.

"Don't worry. My blood isn't drugged."

His blood? He was offering his blood to her again?

She didn't speak, not until they'd reached that little bar again. And, sure enough, lots of Para Unit Agents had swarmed the place.

"Sir—" A man with deep coffee skin rushed toward Eric.

"Assist in rounding up and securing all the werewolves on scene, Lawrence. Collar them. They need one serious silver lockdown."

She shivered. Ella knew all about the collars—silver collars that were placed around a werewolf's neck in order to keep the beast under control. During her captivity with Keegan, she'd heard him raging about those. Anything that made werewolves weak…it had pissed off Keegan.

"And make sure," Eric added, his voice close to a snarl, "that any humans here are briefed with our standard cover story."

"Yes, sir!" The fellow hurried away.

"Cover story?" Ella asked. She was so weak. That gold netting had hurt her badly. Now Eric would know of her weakness. Silver hurt werewolves, and gold weakened her kind. Would he immediately fashion a gold net to trap her? No doubt, his men would retrieve the net from the woods. But maybe they wouldn't stop with just a net. The Para Unit was so clever. No, *Eric* was clever. Maybe he'd just create a golden collar to control her, too.

I have to get away from him.

Unfortunately, her vow wouldn't make it easy.

Once her kind gave a vow, they were compelled to keep it. Whether that vow was for good or evil, it *would* be done.

"The cover story is a gas leak. They happen, you know." He held her easily as he walked toward a black SUV that waited a good distance away from the bar. "People get light-headed and they imagine all kinds of things after an exposure. Gas, carbon monoxide. We toss out different explanations to vary things up."

Her lips twisted. "Humans don't believe that."

He paused and glanced down at her. She hadn't noticed just how strong and hard his jaw was, not until that moment. "It's easier to believe that. Safer. Gas leaks can be explained. You don't have to fear them, twenty-four seven. But real-life monsters with super human strength? Most humans *don't* want to believe in them, so they just…don't."

Denial. Yes, she supposed that had helped to keep the paranormals secret for so long.

"What in the hell…?"

That sharp voice drew her gaze to the right. Connor was there, standing just beside the now open passenger door of the SUV.

"What happened to her?" Connor asked.

She felt the breeze on her shoulders. Ella glanced down. Her shirt was pretty much gone. Her wings had just cut right through the back, and when she'd shifted that second time—returning to what she thought of as semi-normal—the back had been shredded again. It wasn't a big surprise that the fabric had fallen away. At least she was still wearing her bra. Mostly. And even as she had that thought, the bra fell. *Hell.*

Connor's eyes had turned to slits as he stared at her exposed skin. "Are those *burn* marks?"

Oh. He hadn't been focused on her nudity. Made sense. The guy was mated and all. She'd seen his mate the night he'd pulled her from that basement. Connor's mate had nearly died, and he'd pretty much gone insane before Ella's eyes.

I wanted to repay my debt to him, so I gave the woman my blood.

"They are burns," Eric said, his voice hard. "Those werewolves were waiting with a gold net to trap her."

"Why would gold hurt her?" Connor asked.

She almost rolled her eyes. Why would silver hurt a werewolf? *It just does.* No, actually, there was a reason. Precious metals had great power within them. Enough power to chain nearly any beast.

"I don't know," Eric said. "But I will be finding out." Then he put her on the passenger seat. She'd avoided looking at her arms because she hadn't wanted to see those burns, but now her gaze fell. Dark, red lines cut across her skin. Over and over. And—

Eric yanked off his shirt and—very gently—he put it over her, covering her upper body. "Leave us alone, Connor," he ordered, his voice brisk. "You supervise the team out here. Make sure every werewolf in the vicinity is rounded up and brought in for containment."

"Right." Connor hurried away.

Ella swallowed and glanced up at Eric. "What happens now?" *Not back to containment. Not back to—*

"Will fresh blood make those marks go away?"

"Healing will, yes."

He offered his wrist to her. Just…right there. With his agents swarming all around. She knew there was supposed to be a stigma associated with the vamp bite. Most people sure didn't offer themselves up as blood donors to the undead. Not willingly—they took some convincing. Or, in the case of frat boys, some drinking and flirting.

She didn't understand him. "Eric?"

"I don't want you in pain anymore." Each word seemed torn from him. "Take the blood."

Her fingers rose and curled around his wrist. But she didn't bring his wrist—and his tempting blood—closer to her mouth. Not yet. "Why does my pain matter to you?" It certainly hadn't mattered to anyone else before.

His gaze seemed to darken as he stared at her. "I don't know, but it does. You can't hurt. Not while I'm near. I won't let it happen."

The way he was talking…no, no, it couldn't be. *Not him. Not me. It won't happen.*

"Drink from me," Eric said. "Do it now."

The way he was hunched over her…maybe no one would be able to tell what they were doing. It might just look as if he were tending to her wounds. Not offering his blood to her.

She brought his hand to her mouth. Her tongue licked against his wrist, a move that she hadn't planned.

His breath hissed out.

And her teeth sank into him.

Their gaze held as she drank. His blood was just as rich and hot as before—just as addictive, but she made herself only take a few sips. She just needed a little…

The wave of desire she felt for him took her off-guard. The white-hot need that pulsed through her veins wasn't supposed to happen. She wasn't supposed to taste him and just want.

But she did. Her heart raced. Her breasts tightened. Her sex grew wet.

Wrong place. Wrong man.

So why did he feel so right?

I am in serious trouble.

"Ella…" His voice was gravel-rough, and she knew desire when she heard it. A rough lust that made her ache inside.

Her tongue slid over his wrist once more and she pulled back. Her breath was coming too fast, and her teeth were still too sharp.

"We're going to be together," Eric said as he still leaned inside the passenger door. "We both know that."

Ella shook her head. "No, you—" She stopped as shame burned through her.

"I—what?"

"It's just the bite. It makes you want me. It's the way it's designed." Ella didn't want a lover that way. She wanted a man who desired her—no strings attached. No addictive bite needed.

He laughed, and the sound seemed to slide right over her, making her shiver. Not with fear, but with something a whole lot hotter. "It's not the bite. I wanted you long before you took your first taste of me." His eyes glinted. "Now I wonder, when will I get a taste of you?"

Her breath caught.

Eric's jaw locked and he backed up. Then he shut the passenger door. She watched him march around to the front of the vehicle. His voice was strong as he called out orders to his team. More vehicles were arriving. Containment was in full effect there.

She glanced down at her arms. Ella pushed his shirt aside. The burns were already fading as his blood gave her power. Too much power.

What is he? She'd spent so many years protecting her own secrets that she'd forgotten there were other beings out there like her.

Hope began to stir within her. Maybe, just maybe…Eric could be the one she'd been waiting for. So many years. Was it even possible?

Ella glanced through the windshield. He was staring at her. She pulled his shirt back up, inhaling his scent with a pleasure she shouldn't feel.

He knew about the bond formed from a promise. He wasn't controlled by my bite.

She couldn't take her gaze off him.

Maybe…maybe Eric knew so much because he was just like her.

Finally…a mate? Was it even possible?

He stalked around the car. Climbed into the driver's seat. And he started to crank the engine. Her hand flew out and her fingers wrapped around his. "Don't lock me up again."

He stared down at her hand. Did he feel the heat surge when they touched? She did, and she'd never felt anything like that before. It was off the charts. It was *amazing*…

And, again, the tempting thought danced through her mind once more…

Mate.

Impossible. Wasn't it?

"I won't," Eric said. "I won't lock you up."

Her breath eased out.

He cranked the ignition. She kept touching him. She should stop that. She didn't. "Where are we going?"

"I'm taking you home."

That one word was so bittersweet to her. Longing and pain filled Ella, and she didn't speak again as they pulled away.

***

Keegan James stared down at his skin. Angry burns ravaged his body. There wasn't a place on him that the fire hadn't touched. He'd been trapped in that house, a prisoner in the basement as the fire had closed in on him. He'd burned and shifted, over and over in a vicious cycle, as he fought to survive. Eventually, he'd stopped being able to shift. Eventually, he'd stopped being able to heal.

Eventually the fire had stopped.

He'd managed to crawl away then. Every move had been agony. Every move was still agony. He should have been dead. He knew it. He'd survived for one reason alone—

Ella.

Her blood. She'd made him powerful. For a time, he'd been *all* powerful. And then the Para Unit had tracked him down. They'd taken Ella.

They'd tried to kill him.

Try harder next time.

Slowly, he walked toward the window and stared out into the night. The clothes scraped against his burns—hurting him. Everything *hurt.* He knew he looked like a monster. The real stuff of nightmares. He'd tried to call up his beast, but the wolf was silent.

Dead.

But Keegan thought the beast could be born again. If he just had the right tool. And that tool…it was Ella. Magical Ella. His men were out hunting for her even then. He would catch her again. Catch her, cage her, keep her…until he'd taken every single last bit of power from her.

He would be whole again. No matter what he had to do.

The Para Unit wouldn't win. Ella wouldn't escape.

And he'd be more than a monster.

CHAPTER FIVE

"This…this isn't home." Ella's voice sounded disappointed as she stared up at the sprawling warehouse. "You lied to me."

He tensed. "Actually, no, I didn't. This is where I live." And, yes, it wasn't cozy and it wasn't exactly the best neighborhood in the world, but he didn't live a normal life.

Eric waved to the guard and the gates in front of the warehouse opened.

"This isn't home," Ella said once more. Her voice was harder now. "This is another Para Unit facility, isn't it? Jeez, how many of those places do you have?"

Too many. But the exact number was classified. Instead of answering her, Eric said, "I have an apartment here. My home." Pretty much the only one he had these days. "Until we can sort things out, you'll be staying there." He followed the drive that led into the warehouse. And once they were inside and the heavy doors closed behind them…

It's not a warehouse. It was a sprawling, multi-level facility. His new primary base for the Para Unit. All hell had been breaking loose in the last few months, and he'd had to regroup with his agents. This place had the highest security. Sure, it was no Purgatory, but it was still pretty damn impenetrable. Werewolves were housed four levels below, kept absolutely secure until their transports. The top two levels were for agents—some apartments, regular offices, even a cafeteria. The FBI had actually created the facility years ago—back when the werewolf situation had first presented itself. Now, the place was finally getting some serious usage.

While they had driven, Ella had pushed her arms through the sleeves of his shirt and loosely buttoned the front. The shirt seemed to swallow her delicate frame as she sat beside him. He'd killed the engine, but she made no move to get out of the vehicle.

"This isn't the place I was before."

"No." This facility was much closer to the Canadian border.

"Just how many containment areas do you have?"

Ah, she was back to that, huh? He opened his door and hurried around to her side of the vehicle. He inclined his head to the nearby guards. Then Eric pulled open her door. When she rose, the sweet scent of lilacs drifted to his nose. *How the hell does she still smell like that?* He cleared his throat. "I can't tell you how many areas we possess. That's classified."

Her laughter was soft and a little bitter. "I forgot. I'm the enemy. I don't get to know—"

His fingers curled around her wrist. "Is that what you are? The enemy? I'd thought we had a deal. That we were working on the same side now."

Before she could speak, he turned and headed toward the elevator. He kept his hold on her wrist and Eric used his keycard to have those elevator doors sliding open. Most of the apartments were on this floor, but his…

He pushed the button to head down. Three floors.

"You won't have to worry about sunlight."

"I never do."

Her answer was instant and—surprising. But he didn't let his surprise show. Instead, he just said, "Of course not. Sunlight or moonlight. Neither have any influence on you." So he was guessing. He was walking in the dark with her, going on bits of rumors he'd heard over the years. If his suspicions were right, Ella was someone very, very special indeed.

She could be the pivotal piece I need in this struggle.

Because there was a hell of a lot going on in the world right then. Purgatory—oh, but

Purgatory was a serious cluster fuck. One he was still working hard to contain. He'd made a lot of progress recently, but there was still plenty of work to be done at the prison.

He'd tried to warn the powers-that-be about the problems that would come from putting all of the most powerful supernatural beings in one small area.

They could join together. They could become even more dangerous.

But his warnings had been ignored. Of course, he'd learned—too late—that one of the senators pushing for Purgatory had *wanted* all of that chaos to break loose. The guy had possessed illusions of grandeur when it came to the paranormal world. Senator Donald Quick had thought that he'd become a powerful werewolf. He'd believed the paranormals were poised to take over and to come out to the humans.

He'd been wrong.

Now, he was also dead.

But the battle wasn't over. There were still secret groups out there, dangerous factions who wanted to rip the veil of secrecy away from the paranormals. They wanted the humans to know about them. To know and be terrified.

But terror would only create more violence. That *wasn't* the way. Balance had to be maintained.

And, sometimes, it took monsters to create that balance.

"Uh, Eric? The elevator stopped."

He blinked. His left hand ran over his face. Damn but he was tired. He'd been on her trail for the last forty-eight hours, and he'd barely slept. He'd been too…worried about her.

He stepped forward. His right hand was still curled around her wrist.

They passed a few guards. He saw the curious glances thrown his way. So what if it looked as if he were holding her hand? And…

Shit, I don't have a shirt on.

For the first time in far longer than he could remember, Eric felt himself flush.

"Are you blushing?" Her voice was a hushed whisper. "You are. Oh, my—"

His keycard swiped over his lock. He leaned forward, did a retinal scan, and the door opened. Eric hurriedly pulled Ella inside.

She was smiling. Laughing softly. The sound was oddly beautiful.

"The big, bad Para Unit director. Blushing because—"

"Because it looks as if I had sex with you on the way here?" Him—no shirt. Her—disheveled hair and wearing *his* missing shirt. No wonder they'd gotten curious glances. Curious and knowing. Hell.

Her mouth dropped. Then closed. "Oh. That's what they—you're director! Can't you tell them to stop thinking that? Order them to?" Now she sounded insulted and scandalized.

She didn't really need to sound that insulted. It was rough on his ego.

He shut the door behind them. "Take off the shirt."

Ella whirled toward him. "What?"

Through gritted teeth he said, "I'm not asking for a strip tease." Perhaps it had sounded that way. And in his mind, he knew that would be awesome, but…"I just want to check your wounds. We have other doctors on staff here." Though he thought Holly was the best. "If necessary, I can have one of them come in and check you out." He'd never forget the way she'd looked, huddled on the ground beneath that net. Her body had shuddered in pain and he—

He'd never wanted to kill anyone more.

Those bastards were swarming me. They were trying to take her from me. I would have killed them all before I let them take her.

Hardly civilized thoughts. Especially for a man who was always supposed to have his control in place. But that night, his control had started to crack.

Her blue gaze cut away from his. "You gave me your blood. I'm okay."

"I need to see for myself." Both her wounds—and her wings. When he'd seen her fly…everything had changed for him. He'd witnessed plenty during his time as director of the Para Unit. Hell, he'd seen plenty *before* he'd taken the director's position. He hadn't thought he could be shocked any longer. He'd been wrong.

"Fine." Her hands went to the line of buttons on the front of his shirt. Perhaps it was his imagination, but her fingers seemed to be trembling a bit as she unhooked the buttons. Then she opened the shirt and let it fall to the floor. "There? Happy." She held her arms out in front of her body. "The marks have faded. I'm as good as new."

Not quite. He could still see faint red lines on her body. The pain she must have been feeling…all of those burns. Eric crossed to her side in an instant, pulled there, helplessly.

His hand lifted toward her.

"What—what are you doing?" Suspicion flashed on her face.

His fingers skimmed over her shoulder. "Does it hurt when I touch you?" His fingers hesitated over one red mark that circled her shoulder.

"No." She licked her lips. "There's no pain now. Humans would say it wasn't even like a mild sunburn."

His fingers started to lower to her skin, but he stopped, and his hand fisted.

"Eric?"

His head bent and his lips brushed over her shoulder. He felt her whole body stiffen. "I don't like..." Eric kissed her shoulder again. "For you to be in pain."

"I don't like it either," she whispered.

He lifted her arm. There was another faint red line—this one was on the inside of her elbow. He pressed his mouth to that mark.

"You don't have to do that." Her words sounded rushed. "No, I mean, you shouldn't be doing that. Don't. I'm okay now. Really."

But she hadn't been okay before. She'd been crying. "I wasn't sure I'd get to you." He brought her wrist to his mouth. Another red mark was there. He remembered when she'd grabbed the net and it had pressed to her hands. She'd screamed.

She screamed for me.

And something inside of him had roared back for her.

"I thought you were dead when those werewolves swarmed you." Her voice was softer than a breath, but his enhanced hearing easily picked up her words. "I didn't want you to die."

He brought her wrist to his mouth. He pressed his lips to her wrist. Felt the fast and frantic pounding of her pulse.

Why did people believe that vampires were cold? That their hearts didn't beat? They still lived—their hearts had to beat. If they didn't, they'd just be decomposing piles of flesh. Zombies, not vamps.

Though he hadn't encountered any actual zombies yet, and of all the paranormal creatures out there, Eric was sure hoping that those guys were just myths. Stories to frighten children.

And men.

Ella's heart beat. It pounded in a beautiful rhythm. His mouth pressed to her delicate wrist and his lips parted because it would be so very easy—incredibly so—to sink his teeth into her skin.

No. You have rules. You have control. Keep it in place.

"Eric?"

He lifted his head. Were his fangs showing? He rarely let them out. But then, his relationship with Ella was going to be different. She wasn't like the others.

His gaze slid over her. Ella's breasts thrust toward him. Beautiful, small, but perfectly rounded—actually absolutely perfect. Dark tips. Tight. Tempting. Would she moan when he tasted them? When he licked them?

His cock shoved against the front of his jeans. The damn thing was so heavy and full that he was afraid he'd bust his zipper at any moment.

He couldn't ever remember wanting a woman the way he wanted her. Was it because of her bite?

Was it just because she was…Ella?

"Turn around," he said, sounding far too rough and hard. But if she didn't turn around, her nipple would be in his mouth in the next five seconds.

Five.

Four.

Three.

Two –

Her hand slipped from his and she turned.

His eyes snapped closed and he concentrated on breathing. Slow and deep. Slow. Deep. *The way I want to fuck her.*

His eyes flew right back open.

There were more faint red marks on her back but—where her wings had been before, there was nothing. No raised flesh to mark them. No difference at all in her skin or her bone structure. His index finger slid along the ridge of her left shoulder blade, and she shivered.

"Does my touch bother you?" Eric asked her.

"No." She glanced over her shoulder at him. "I like it…too much."

He didn't breathe for a moment. He was busy using all of his will power and *not* jumping her.

"Am I supposed to pretend that I don't want you?" Ella laughed and the husky sound rolled right over his skin as if she'd just touched his body. "I'm standing in front of you, naked from the waist up. You can see me—there's no hiding. Yes, I like it when you touch me. Yes, I want you to touch me more." But she pulled away from him. She grabbed for the shirt she'd tossed aside moments before and now she held it up in front of her body, as if it were some sort of shield. "The problem is that I don't know if I can trust you."

His hands clenched into fists. He missed the silk of her skin. And he really didn't like that she'd covered up those gorgeous breasts.

"You should be demanding to know what I am." Her chin lifted. "Asking me where my wings went. Asking—like Connor did—why the gold hurt me. There are a million questions you *should* be asking me, and instead, you ask if your touch bothers me…*bothers me,*" she repeated with a rough shake of her head. "If you're the one, then isn't your touch supposed to make me react that way? Isn't it supposed to make me need you so much that I can barely hold back?"

He could see her desire for him, flashing in her gaze. A dull roar filled his own ears. He'd held back for so long, always pretending to have ice in his veins. But she was different.

He was different.

"When you look at me," Ella continued, "what do you think?"

"I think I want you naked, and I want to taste every single inch of you." Brutal honesty.

Her breath heaved out. "I thought I was your prisoner."

"I was keeping you *safe.*"

"Safety can look a lot prison to someone with my past."

He needed her to trust him, with every secret that she had. Because he'd realized just how important she was in this twisted game he played. "I'm not planning to send you to prison."

Her eyes seemed bigger. Bluer. "Are you sure? Because I've got it on pretty good authority that you do that. I mean, your whole job is about sending paranormals to Purgatory, isn't it?"

He didn't want to ever think of Ella in Purgatory. The bastards there would tear her apart. *Never.*

Eric took a step toward her.

She lifted her hand, the gesture telling him to stop. "I don't think well enough when you get too close. Maybe it's your blood…"

"Did you like the way I taste?"

"Yes."

"I don't normally offer myself up like that, just so you know.'

Her gaze searched his. "Then why am I so different?"

His stare fell to her mouth. Her bottom lip was fuller than her top. Plump. Sexy. Biteable. "You tell me."

"Eric…"

"I really like that," he told her. "When you say my name that way, it makes me want all kinds of things…"

She backed up a step.

"But all I want tonight…" Despite the huge dick that was shoving through his pants. "I want to kiss you, Ella."

"Kiss me?"

"Just kiss you. One kiss so I can see how you taste."

Now her eyes were on his mouth. He'd controlled himself—and forced his fangs away.

"One kiss," she said. "I think I'd like that." Then she laughed again. Her laughter did something to him. His chest ached and he felt—hell, less hollow on the inside. "A kiss from you seems like a perfect way to end this insane night."

He closed the space between them. Ella tipped back her head as she stared up at him. One of her hands still held his shirt pressed to her chest.

Her lips were parted.

So perfect.

His hand lifted and curled under her chin. His head lowered and his mouth closed over hers.

Slowly, slowly…

Her tongue licked over his lips.

Fuck slow.

Desire burst beyond his control. White-hot. Burning him from the inside out. His left arm wrapped around her and he pulled her closer while his right tipped her head back even more. Her lips were parted fully for him, and his tongue thrust past her lips. He tasted her. One taste.

Eric knew he would crave no one else.

Better than wine. Rich and sweet and decadent all at the same time. He feasted on her. The shirt fell away and he felt the tips of her breasts press against his chest. She was pulling him closer, and closer was the only place he wanted to be.

In his mind, he could see them together. Twined on the bed. Naked. He was driving into her again and again. They rolled across that bed. Her body held his cock like a tight, hot glove. She rose above him and her wings spread out behind her as she came, gasping his—

Ella pulled away from him. Her breath heaved out. Her whole body shook. And there was a bright flush on her cheeks.

It took him a moment to realize he wasn't in bed with her. He wasn't *in* her. His teeth clenched to hold back a snarl of fury because he wanted her so badly. The fantasy had taken over his mind. He'd been able to feel her against him. Feel what it was like to be *in* her.

"Are you…the one I waited for?" Ella asked him.

He had no fucking clue what she was talking about. But Eric knew that if he didn't get away from her, he'd be taking her. Right. Then.

He spun away.

"Eric!" She touched his shoulder.

Desire—dark and demanding—filled his blood. "Unless you want to fuck, right there on that bed, *now,* you'll let me go." Talking was hard, but she needed to understand. "You do something to me…" His voice sounded like a beast. Like a werewolf in mid-shift. Half man. Half animal. "I don't think the way I want you is…normal." Not normal. Not safe. "Dangerous."

He was just realizing that now.

Her hand slid away. He marched for the door. His gaze zeroed in on the door. He just focused on it, focused on putting one foot in front of the other. He was almost there—

"I don't mind dangerous," Ella said. "In fact, I rather like it."

Sonofa—

He yanked open the door and headed out before the last thread of his control shredded.

***

Ella's hand lifted and she touched her lips. He'd kissed her—and it had been wild, rough, perfect. She'd gotten lost with him, so caught up, imagining what it would be like if he took her to bed. If he took her.

Her clothes would have been gone. His would have been across the room. He would have sunk deep into her. She would have ridden him and the pleasure would have slammed into them both.

The fantasy had been so real. She'd never kissed a man and wanted him that badly. Never kissed a man and *seen* what it would be like to be with him.

For a second there, she'd even thought she'd felt the hard press of his fangs against her.

Ella stared at that shut door, and for the first time in centuries, real hope flooded through her. He could truly be the one.

Her footsteps padded toward that door. She reached for the knob. Tried to turn it. He could be—

He'd locked her inside.

She yanked on that door, trying to jerk the thing open, but it didn't give at all. Her eyes narrowed as she studied that whole door. It wasn't wood but some kind of reinforced metal. Was it that paranormal-proof stuff supposedly used at Purgatory? Why would the guy paranormal-proof his own room?

To keep the monsters out?

Or to…keep his own monster in?

***

Eric grabbed a t-shirt from the stock room and yanked it on. It was a damn good thing they kept spare uniforms there because he couldn't face Ella again. Not yet. He needed to get his desire for her back under control.

The shirt was a little too tight as it stretched across his shoulders, but it would have to do for the moment.

He headed to prisoner transport and watched as the werewolves were brought in. Each prisoner had already been collared. Most of them were unconscious. All but the one with the scar.

Eric's gaze zeroed in on the fellow. "That's the guy," he murmured to the guards near him. "Get that fellow set up for a little chat."

"Right away…" The agent started to turn, but then he hesitated. "Boss, are you okay? You just…you look different."

Automatically, Eric put his hand up to his mouth. His fangs weren't out. No, of course, they weren't. "Just pissed off, Lawrence," he said. "I don't like it when a pack attacks a woman and leaves her crying on the ground. That bastard—" He pointed to the scarred wolf.

"He was the one in charge tonight. He *will* be telling me everything I want to know."

Lawrence Carter, one of the newer agents but one who was proving to have a serious knack for the job, nodded quickly, "Yes, sir. I'll get him ready for you."

Lawrence hurried away and as he left, the guy nearly plowed right into Connor. Growling, Connor shouldered Lawrence back, then he closed in on Eric.

"What the hell is going on?" Connor asked.

"Keegan."

Connor's face hardened. "A dead man isn't an issue for me."

Actually, he was. And since the bastard in question was Connor's blood, Eric couldn't hold back with him. "I told you before, I'm not sure he's dead. Unless I have remains, I'm not sure." His heart was pounding too fast, and he could still smell lilacs. "Those men were waiting. They knew Ella would come after them. They picked a remote spot, and just…bided their damn time."

"They knew she'd catch their scent."

He nodded. "I think that scarred asshole there—he must have been part of the group that originally took her."

"You mean you don't know?" Connor asked. "Hell, man, what have you been doing if not questioning her?"

Nearly fucking her. "Building trust," Eric snapped. "It's an art, okay?" He and Connor hadn't started with the best of relationships—mostly because Eric *might* have sent the guy to Purgatory. But things had changed between them. He now considered Connor his friend. Connor didn't have to work for the Para Unit any longer—he'd repaid his debts—but the guy had stuck around because he understood the battle they were facing.

Connor knew—first-hand—just how dangerous paranormals could be when they went out of control. He had the marks to prove that, delivered courtesy of his own father.

"Right, an art," Connor nodded.

Eric growled at him.

"Dude, you are sounding way too much like a beast. Maybe you need a werewolf break—before you start shifting just like we do."

Connor didn't understand his secrets. Friend or not, there were some things Eric didn't share. "I'm bringing Shane in on this case."

"The vamp?" Connor whistled. "Calling in the big guns, are you?"

"Shane August has been around for a very long time." More years than most could ever guess. "I need his input on Ella."

"Your winged vampiress." Connor nodded. "Got to say, I've seen some trippy shit in my time, but I've never seen a vamp with wings, until tonight."

Your winged vampiress. "She's not mine," Eric said as he turned and headed down the corridor that would take him to the interrogation room.

"But you want her to be..."

Eric stilled and glanced back at Connor. Laughing, Connor touched his nose. "Seriously, man. You know we all have enhanced senses. You smell like you bathed in lilacs."

He could feel himself flushing. Seriously—blushing twice in one damn day? This shit was stopping. "Do not fucking push me."

Connor just grinned.

"Where's Chloe?" Eric asked, changing the topic before he had to punch the guy. "Because the last thing we want is this pack seeing her."

That wiped the grin right off Connor's face. "They aren't touching her." Connor delivered those words with lethal certainty. "She's miles away from here, and that's the way it's staying until we figure out what's going on."

If they found out that Keegan was alive, they'd have to take steps to protect Chloe. Keegan had been obsessed with her before. And Connor—well, he was in love with her. "Fucking mates," Eric muttered. "Why is that such a big deal in the paranormal world? Mates and bonding and shit that makes my head want to explode."

"Chloe is *not* Keegan's mate." That lethal intensity had sharpened even more. "He's a delusional bastard. Chloe belongs with me."

Too bad Keegan hadn't gotten that message. At least, he hadn't until they'd burned a house down on the fellow.

"The prisoner should be secured now," Eric said, giving a firm nod. "Let's do this damn thing."

***

Keegan threw his phone across the room. No one had checked in. The pack knew they were supposed to contact him. They followed orders. *Always.*

Fury beat within him and a sinister voice seemed to whisper in his mind…

Maybe they aren't following your orders any longer because they think you're weak. You can't transform. If you have no beast, they won't respect you.

He'd once sought a mate who hadn't been able to fully shift. He hadn't thought of that as a weakness for her. She'd still kept the beast's strength while in human form. He'd thought that Chloe was the next step in werewolf evolution.

But he…

I have no enhanced strength. I have burns and pain and hell.

"Come back," he snarled into the night. His men should have contacted him, dammit. They only wouldn't have checked in if…

If they decided to keep Ella for themselves. They know of her power. Maybe they want it.

Or…

The Para Unit had Ella. Maybe she's working with them now. Maybe she trapped my men.

Neither possibility was a good one.

Keegan marched to the gun cabinet. He loaded silver bullets into his weapon. First one gun, then another. If his pack had turned, he'd put them out of their misery.

And if Ella was trying to play him…

He'd show her the error of her ways.

CHAPTER SIX

The werewolf was collared and sat at the narrow, wooden table, a glare twisting his face.

Eric headed toward the table and took his time sitting down in the chair across from the guy. He saw the werewolf's nostrils flare and the fellow's eyes glinted.

"Ella…" The wolf whispered.

Connor had been right. The others were picking up her scent on him. If she'd marked him, had he marked her?

I hope so.

"No wonder," the werewolf's voice was a growl, "you came in with guns blazing. Tried to take your new pet, did we?"

"She's hardly a pet."

The werewolf's hand lifted to the silver collar that circled him. "Get this fucking thing off me."

The collar's remote control rested comfortably in Eric's hand. "What's your name?"

"Get it—"

Eric pressed a button on the control.

"Fucking hell!" The werewolf's breath hissed out. "Reece. It's Reece."

"Got a last name?" Eric was aware of Connor entering the room. From the corner of his eye, he saw Connor lean against the right wall and cross his arms over his chest.

"No, I'm like damn Madonna," Reece muttered. "And don't shock me again!"

Eric looked at the remote. "I didn't shock you. Don't you understand how the collars work? Silver is in there. Liquid silver. And when then remote is used, that silver is injected into your blood through tiny needles that line the collar." He looked back up at the prisoner.

Reece's eyes had gone wide.

"Really, I thought you'd understand more about how this all worked. Keegan knew about the tech we had here. Why would he keep you in the dark?"

Reece smiled. "The dead can't talk. So he wouldn't—"

"This is how it's going to work." Eric gave the fellow a smile of his own. One that he knew was cold and cruel. "I don't have time to waste. So if you don't want to cooperate with me, there are plenty of other werewolves in there who do. The first one who talks is going to get better treatment from the Para Unit. Maybe that one won't rot in Purgatory. We'll just have to see…"

Reece's jaw had hardened. "I'm not afraid of Purgatory."

"Why? Because Keegan told you he had control in there?" Eric shook his head. "*I* have control there now. Full authority. Things have changed. My men took over. You go there, and you're gone."

The werewolf's breathing seemed to get faster.

"I know a scar caused by claw marks when I see one." Eric tilted his head as he studied the marks on Reece's face. "But because werewolves heal so well…I'm guessing you had to get that scar when you were a lot younger. Maybe even before your first shift."

Reece wasn't talking.

So Eric just kept going. "You're in a pack, so I figure one of your pack mates gave it to you. Seeing as how Keegan is such a twisted, sadistic SOB, I bet it was him. Was he punishing you? Did you try to break the rules and Keegan snapped your ass back into shape?"

Still, nothing.

"So now, you protect him." Eric shook his head. "Don't see why the hell you should. This is your chance to be free of him. Tell me where he is, and I'll make sure he's out of your pack for good."

Reece glanced from Eric to Connor.

"Tell me…" Eric said.

Disgust filled Reece's face. "I don't turn on my pack. Someone like you would never understand that. You can't."

Bullshit. The Para Unit was his pack. His family. And he would do anything to protect his agents. What he wouldn't do—kill innocents for them. "Think about it. You have five minutes to make the decision to talk or that deal is gone."

"What—"

"Why did you go after Ella?" Eric fired out the question.

Reece licked his lips. "Why do you want to fuck her? Cause she's hot and—"

"Pissing me off isn't to your advantage." His voice was soft but fury had roared through him. "You knew the type of net to use on her. You were just waiting, weren't you? Because you thought she'd come looking for you."

Reece's thick brows lifted. "Is that what she told you? She has been here with you, right? Getting all cozy. Seducing you so you'd be on her side."

He'd tried to seduce her, but Ella had backed away. Desire still had him tense, and the jerk across the table was about to feel the full brunt of his fury.

"Do you even know what she is?" Reece taunted. "Or has she already taken your blood and told you what to think?"

Connor's arms dropped to his sides.

Eric laughed. "Don't worry. I'm not under anyone's control."

"You sure came running fast after her." Reece leaned forward. "Is she that good of a screw? I always wondered. I mean, I know she's supposed to be waiting for her own kind and all that shit. But like it was gonna happen. She's the last, isn't she?"

He knows what she is. And for that reason, Eric didn't rip Reece's throat out. Yet.

"Yes," Eric said softly, playing along. "She's the last, and that's why Keegan wants her, right? Why he will do anything possible to get her back. He was stronger than he should have been, because he took her blood."

Reece laughed. "We had to keep her starved or there would have been no controlling her. The first night, we got lucky. Caught her with the net then slashed her with our claws. She bled fast."

Every muscle in Eric's body tightened. "Connor, leave now."

"Uh, boss, I don't know…"

"Leave."

Connor headed out.

Eric waited for the door to shut. "Do you enjoy hurting women?"

"Not like she's human. She can take the pain." Reece smirked at him. "Maybe she even liked it."

He wanted to push the button to send a maximum silver dosage into the bastard. "I don't think she did."

Reece shrugged.

"You kept her starved and chained – gold was in the chains, right? Because that would have made those burn marks on her wrists. You and your pack kept her there for Keegan because you'd learned just what she was."

Reece kept that stupid smirk on his face. The fool did not realize the danger he faced.

"After you'd made her transform Keegan…" Because that was exactly what they'd done. They'd forced blood exchanges between Ella and Keegan, he knew that. And Keegan had become something far more than just a werewolf. "What were you going to do? Kill her?"

Reece leaned forward. "No, we were going to let her *think* she'd escaped. We needed her wings to come back out, see."

Now the bastard was chatty. Because he thought it was safe to talk about Ella and not Keegan? *He won't turn on his alpha.* Now Eric was even more convinced that Keegan was still alive. After all, if the guy was dead, Reece would just say so. Instead, he was doing everything he could to take the focus off Keegan. And that everything involved telling all about the hell he'd put Ella through during her captivity.

But the fool didn't know that each word was pushing Eric closer and closer to the edge.

Ella…in pain.

Ella…bleeding.

Ella…starving…

Ella…dying?

"Once the wings were out, we would've used our claws to cut them off her. We would have—*Ah!*" Reece screamed in agony.

"Oh, sorry." Eric glance down at the remote. "I guess my finger slipped."

Reece kept screaming. He'd lurched out of his chair and was straining and twisting as he tried to find relief from the silver onslaught.

"Whoops. It's still slipping. How about that?" He could taste fury burning in his mouth as he focused on Reece once more. "Maybe we should get a few things straight here. One, you are never *ever* supposed to so much as even look at Ella again. If you do, I will push so much silver into your blood that you will still be hurting even when you're roasting in hell."

Reece's screams bounced off the walls.

"Two," Eric said, voice grim and cold, "no one touches her wings. No one touches *her*. If they do, I'll fucking kill them." That warning came from deep inside. Primal. Instinctive.

No one would hurt her again.

His finger eased off the remote.

Reece had fallen to the floor.

Eric took a deep breath. *Can't kill him. Can't kill the bastard. I'm supposed to be the one delivering justice. He'll go to Purgatory. He'll be judged and punished just like any other criminal and –*

Reece was laughing again. "Dumb…human. You can only…hurt me…with that stupid box."

The box? The remote?

Reece lifted up his head. "Why don't you try coming at me…one on one…see how tough you are then?"

Eric's heart beat faster. "I was really hoping you'd say some stupid shit like that. I mean, if you ask for an ass whipping, all I can do is oblige." He headed across the room and put the remote down, well out of the werewolf's reach.

Then he stood there and rolled back his shoulders as Reece climbed back to his feet.

"Just so we're clear," Eric said. "When we're done and you beg me to stop…"

We would've used our claws to cut them off her…

Eric's hands fisted. "After the guards drag you back to your cell, word is going to spread to the other werewolves that you talked about Keegan. That you told me everything."

Reece's eyes widened.

"And we'll see just how much that pack accepts you then."

"You bastard – you can't – "

"Then you'd better talk. Because they'll think you did, no matter what." Playing dirty? Yes, he excelled at it.

Reece started running toward him.

"Maybe after the ass whipping, you'll get chatty," Eric said. Reece's hand flew toward his face, but Eric caught the guy's wrist and stopped him. "Something else you should know," Eric said as he easily held the guy. "I never said I was human." Then he slammed his head into Reece's face.

***

Twenty minutes later, Eric marched out of the interrogation room. Connor straightened when he saw him. "Uh, Eric…"

"Give him five minutes, then take him back with the others. Let it be known that he just came out of a long sit-down with me."

Connor's gaze swept over him. "There's blood on your shirt," he said.

Eric glanced down. "Huh. How about that? It's not mine." He moved to step around Connor.

Connor blocked his way. "And I can see your fangs."

Eric stilled. His tongue slid over and sure enough, he could feel the sharp point of a fang. His gaze shot to Connor's. *So much for that damn secret.*

"Do I need to get Holly?"

He was lucky no other agents were around. Connor might have questions, but the guy wasn't going to ask, not then. Or maybe…maybe he'd suspected the truth about Eric for a while.

"I don't need Holly." His voice was too rough. Way too hard. "I need—" He stopped.

But they both knew what he'd been about to say.

Ella.

"If Reece gets ready to talk, come and get me." He made sure not to flash fang as he shouldered around Connor. "I'm going to crash."

"Is that what you're calling it?" Connor murmured.

"Screw off," Eric threw back. The fangs weren't going away. Adrenaline and fury pounded through him. A dangerous combination that was fraying his control.

We would've cut off her wings with our claws.

His vision darkened and he headed for the elevator.

No, he headed for Ella.

***

When the door opened, Ella immediately shot to her feet. She'd been lounging on Eric's sofa, trying to figure out just how much to tell him about her past and—

"No more secrets. No lies." He stood in the doorway, his shoulders stretching to absolutely fill that space. His eyes glittered at her and she was pretty sure she caught sight of fangs just beneath his sexy lips.

Ella swallowed. "You locked me in."

He shut the door. Locked it once more. "For your safety."

"I don't like being locked up. Don't do it again."

Slowly, deliberately, he stalked toward her. Ella refused to back up.

"Can't make that promise." His voice had never sounded so rough. "When your safety is on the line, I'll do whatever is necessary."

Her gaze slid over him. She knew that scent— "Blood."

"Not mine." He stopped right in front of her. "But I'll wash it off before I touch you. Nothing of them will touch you again."

Unease slid through her. "Eric, what did you do?"

"They were going to cut off your wings."

She flinched, but then her shoulders squared. "I suspected that was Keegan's plan." There had to be a reason he'd kept her alive after he'd taken her blood and made her take his. "Too bad for them, they didn't know how to get the wings to appear."

"You were too weak for them to come out," Eric said. "They came back after you drank from me."

That was certainly one of the reasons. "Your blood is very powerful." *You said no secrets, Eric. So tell me your secrets.*

"It should be." He smiled and, yes, he definitely had fangs. Wickedly sharp fangs. "You think it's easy fighting the paranormals out there? I've taken down more alphas than I can count."

It's him. He's the one. Euphoria and hope made her dizzy. He had to be the one. She wouldn't want him this much if he wasn't, right? And she did want him. Even when she'd been furious at him, the need had been there, simmering below her surface.

"I'm going to wash the blood away." His teeth snapped together. "You're gonna want to…stay away from me for a while."

That was the last thing Ella wanted. "You're the one who came to me."

"I know. Because I can't fucking stay away." His gaze hardened. "So you have to be smarter than me. You know we'll combust if we touch…"

Combust.

"I'll wash the blood away." He pointed to the room on the right. "You go in there and lock the door. I swear, I won't come in after you. Not if you lock that door."

She didn't move. Ella wasn't sure if she could move. Her life had been pain and fear and torment for so very long, but Eric was there now, and he was offering her more. The more she'd nearly stopped hoping to have. "And if I don't lock the door?"

"Oh, sweetheart…"

That gravelly endearment made goosebumps rise on her arms.

"My control is shot to hell. You don't—" His jaw clenched. "You don't want to see me without it. No one does."

Then he turned and made his way toward the bathroom. His movements were jerky.

"Actually," Ella said softly when he reached that door, "I think I do."

***

Keegan saw the SUVs at the old bar. Reece had been there—the other werewolf had picked the place for its remote location. He'd said it would be the perfect spot for an ambush.

They'd thought to ambush Ella when she came looking for them. It only made sense that a blood-thirsty creature like her would come searching for vengeance. After all, the desire for revenge was supposed to be in her blood. Revenge. Fury. Hate.

Everything dark…that was Ella.

But Ella hadn't been the one to get ambushed. He knew those SUVs belonged to the government. Para Agents. They'd been there. Was Ella using them? Or were they using her?

He stayed back, not wanting to risk attracting their attention. There were only two SUVs left at the scene, and there was no sign of his pack.

Keegan figured that these guys must be the clean-up crew. Sooner or later, they'd be done, and then they'd return to their base.

He'd follow.

I'll get my pack. And I'll get her.

His burns ached. His body hurt. And the rage just grew even more within him.

***

He'd turned on the shower. Steam drifted from the bathroom, and Ella found herself heading toward that steam. She stripped as she walked, letting her clothes drop to the floor. There would be no going back after they joined. She knew that. But she didn't want to go back. She'd been alone for so long. She'd stopped realizing just how much she craved contact.

Then she'd met Eric.

And the craving—it had come back.

The bathroom door was partially ajar. Her fingers pressed against the wood, opening the door farther. She could see Eric inside. Or at least, she could see the rough outline of his body through the steamy shower's glass wall. He appeared to be leaning forward. Was his head under the spray of water?

She crept forward and reached out to open the glass door of the shower. It opened soundlessly, and she saw that, yes, the heavy spray was soaking his head. He had one hand propped forward, against the tile, and his other hand—

"I can do that for you," Ella offered. *Really, it would be no trouble at all.*

His shoulders stiffened and in the next second, he was whirling around to face her. Water trickled down his body and her gaze hungrily followed that trail. His abs were amazing—rippling beneath the drops of water. There was so much power in his body. Leashed strength.

"Ella…" He said her name in disbelief.

And his cock. Sweet hell. She wanted him in her. So big and hard and stretching right toward her. Ella licked her lips. "Didn't hear me come in?" She shook her head and stepped into the shower. His gaze was sweeping over her and the only word to describe his expression—*lust*. "I guess you were distracted by—"

He was on her in an instant. Eric pushed her back against the shower wall, and it was cold and hard against her shoulder blades. While he—he was hot. He pinned her there with his body as his mouth took hers. Not softly. No way. Hard and deep and consuming. His hands had locked around her waist, and her breasts thrust against his chest.

His heavy arousal pressed against her. Long and hard and she wanted to part her legs and take him inside. They didn't need preliminaries. She was already turned on for him. She wanted him to thrust deep into her, and Ella didn't want to think—not about anything. She just wanted to ride the wave of pleasure with him and forget everything else in the world.

Why not escape with him?

Why—

His hands were moving. Not down, but up. He'd pulled away from her mouth and now he stared down at her as his fingers slid over her breasts. Her nipples were tight and aching and when he touched them, a moan slipped from her lips.

"No...control..." Eric gritted out.

She smiled at him. "Good." Ella could feel her fangs extending. Sex and bloodlust were always tied for her kind. Twisted all together. Physical desire just amplified her need to taste his blood and her physical desire was sure riding high right then.

He bent and took her nipple into his mouth. The water kept pounding down and she sank her fingers into his wet hair as she arched against him. He was laving her nipple. Licking her. Sucking. Kissing. Driving her desire up ever higher.

He kissed his way to her other breast. Gave the same sensual torment to that nipple. She was moaning and her hips were pushing against him. She wanted to ride him long and deep. Right there. Anywhere.

Her hands slid down his body. She wrapped her fingers around his cock. Stroked him, so thick and wide.

"Ella…" Her name was a warning. She was long past the warning point.

He locked his hands around her waist and lifted her up. Oh, yes, this position was so much better. She wrapped her legs around his hips, putting her sex right against him, then she rocked, moving her clit against that hard shaft again and again. The friction was wild, perfect, and when he put his mouth on her neck, when she felt the score of his teeth against her—

Eric bit her.

She cried out and she came. Just like that—pleasure exploded within her and she climaxed in a hard, shaking rush.

He froze. "What the hell have I done?"

"Do it again," Ella demanded instantly as she fought to catch her breath. "Again, again, *again…"*

But he was carrying her out of the shower. He wasn't sinking into her. He *was* holding her with a grip gone far too tight.

"Eric!" She made her voice a demand. Ripples of pleasure still rushed through her body, but that pleasure was only the start. A sample. She wanted that release again and again and again. Endlessly. Until she went mad from it.

He didn't let her go. He yanked off the water and carried her out of the bathroom. Fine, if he was going to play that way...

Ella kissed his neck. She sucked his skin and she nipped him. When his blood slid over her tongue, she nearly came again.

He staggered. "Ella, I'm trying—trying to hold...on...for you..."

She licked and kissed her way to his ear. "Don't," Ella whispered. "Let go. Fuck me like you want. Fuck me like *I* want."

He lowered her onto the bed. His eyes—they seemed to burn with lust now. His jaw was clenched and red stained his cheeks. He parted her legs and pulled her to the edge of the bed. Then, his fingers thrust into her.

Ella knew he'd find her wet and ready. But she hadn't anticipated that the pleasure would hit her again so viciously at his touch.

"Dangerous..." Eric whispered.

"I don't care," Ella said. "I don't care what you are, *I want you.*"

Then he was positioning his cock at the entrance to her body. His hands caught hers. Their fingers twined together and he pushed her hands back against the mattress. He thrust into her, deep and hard.

Their gazes held. He sank into her, driving balls-deep in one smooth thrust. She lost her breath and didn't care.

He withdrew.

Thrust again.

The fire in his eyes just burned brighter. Her need for him burned deeper.

Again and again, he thrust.

Ella turned her head, offering her neck to him. "Bite…"

"Shouldn't…*can't…*"

"With me," Ella whispered as she closed her eyes and surrendered to the need blazing between them. "There isn't a 'can't'."

His mouth pressed to her neck.

"Do it, Eric." She wanted this so much. Them linked fully, no holding back.

His teeth sank into her.

Her moan filled the air because the pleasure was roaring through her. His hips pistoned against her as he drove toward climax. The bed was squeaking and jerking beneath their bodies and he just moved harder. Deeper—

Then he stiffened, and shuddered against her. She felt his hot release inside of her, and it just amplified her pleasure. Her sex contracted, squeezing him tightly, and his lips slid over her neck. Pressing so lightly.

So tenderly.

Her eyes closed and a smile curved her lips. "That was…worth waiting for," Ella whispered.

He pulled out of her, and she hated that. She really would enjoy another round or ten.

But he was tucking her under the covers. Wrapping his body around hers. Such a sweet gesture. So odd for their kind.

Drowsiness pulled at her. For the first time, she thought she might actually be able to lower her guard and sleep deeply. With his arms around her, she felt safe.

With her eyes still closed, Ella turned toward him. "I'm not alone any longer." She'd found him. After all her searching, she'd found another just like her. She hadn't seen his wings yet, but then, he hadn't been enraged so they wouldn't come out.

"No," Eric's voice was rough. "You aren't."

Her hand slid over his heart. She could feel that fast and hard rhythm. "Why do people think our kind are so evil?"

His heart jerked more beneath her touch.

She thought of the way he'd tucked her under the covers and warmth stole through her. "There is so much more to us than people think."

"A lot more..." His lips brushed across her temple. "Go to sleep, Ella. We'll talk when you wake."

Talk. Right. They could do that. Or maybe they could have lots and lots more sex.

She wanted to know how someone like him had come to be in power at the Para Unit. Though, Ella supposed it made sense. Their kind was so powerful, why not hunt the others? Especially if...well, they may have been responsible for *creating* all of those others so long ago.

Some said they were the original evil.

"Never...wanted to be evil," Ella said.

"You aren't." His immediate reply.

That was nice. Really sweet.

She was still smiling as she slipped into sleep.

***

What in the hell did I just do? Eric stared up at the ceiling, with Ella cuddled close to him.

He'd fucked her, yes. He'd taken Ella's blood.

He *never* took blood. Certainly never during sex. But he hadn't been able to stop himself. And Ella's blood—it had been like sweet candy on his tongue. He hadn't been able to get enough, and pleasure had erupted within him when he'd drank from her.

He'd gotten lost.

Even now, he felt a bit drunk from her blood. His head was spinning, and his fangs were still out. The muscles in his body seemed to be stretching, and he didn't even know what was up with that shit.

What he *did* know…it was that he didn't want to move. That he just wanted to keep laying right there, with Ella in his arms. The scent of lilacs was all around him now, and he pretty much loved that scent. She was soft and warm, and for the first time in longer than he could remember, Eric actually felt at peace.

He tightened his hold on her, and his eyes closed.

CHAPTER SEVEN

She dreamed of deserts. Of gunfire. Of blood and cries that filled the night. She dreamed of choking on her own blood and of feeling her body ice as death swept near.

She saw a man bend before her. A man with eyes that blazed with emotion. He was in the battle. He was bloody. He had fangs. *Vampire.*

He was—death?

"Do you want to live?"

Yes, always, yes.

But then the man was gone. Everything was gone. There was only darkness…

***

Eric dreamed of pain. Of a small basement and restraints that burned and never gave way. He dreamed of a hunger that wouldn't end. Of a sadistic werewolf who laughed as he starved.

"I'll take every bit of power you have. You won't have anything left…"

The werewolf bit him and he screamed as his flesh tore. But he swore, one day, he would get out. He would kill that werewolf.

He would destroy Keegan and every member of his pack.

Keegan's laughter faded and then there was only darkness.

***

A loud pounding yanked Eric from sleep. He awoke with a start, his breath heaving out and his body jerking upright.

I'm not alone.

Ella's soft body slid against his. "What's happening?"

For a moment, he just blinked, lost, as he stared at her. Her thick, dark hair tumbled over her shoulders. Her eyes were so wide and deep.

There she is.

Why the hell did he feel as if he'd just found something he'd lost?

The pounding came again. Eric climbed from the bed. He swiped his hand over his face. "It's probably about Reece. The SOB must have decided to tell me about Keegan." He grabbed a pair of jeans. "Go back to sleep. I'll handle this."

"What?"

But he was already hurrying through the apartment. He unlocked the door, and sure enough, Connor stood on the other side. But Connor wasn't alone. Shane August stood behind him.

That sure was fast.

He'd wanted Shane brought in so he could talk to the guy, but Eric hadn't expected the vampire to be there within the hour. "How'd you get here so soon?" Eric asked.

Shane lifted a brow. "It's after dawn. It took me five hours to get here."

Five hours? Hell, he'd really gone into some kind of deep sleep with Ella. He usually only managed an hour or two of sleep. Because of his modifications, he didn't really need more.

"Reece is begging to talk," Connor told him. "Figured you'd want to come and join that sit-down."

Damn straight.

"But you might want to put on a shirt first. Do us all a damn favor there," Connor added.

Growling, Eric turned away—and found Ella walking toward them.

She'd dressed—in one of his t-shirts that she'd knotted near her waist, and she had on her skirt from earlier—a skirt that showed off her legs to perfection. Her hair tumbled over her shoulders and a faint hint of color lined her cheeks. She looked sexy, wicked hot—and totally like she'd just been in his bed.

And I want her back there, ASAP.

Connor and Shane had gone dead silent behind him.

Ella didn't even glance at the other men. Her gaze was locked fully on Eric. "If Reece is talking about Keegan, I want to be there. You aren't shutting me out again." She stalked toward him, stopping only when they were less than a foot apart. "And you're *not* locking me in this room again, either. Getting locked up wasn't part of our deal."

For just a moment, he had a flash of another place. A dusty, smelly basement. No light. Just bugs crawling on the floor. And chains that wouldn't break. *I'll take every bit of power that you have.*

"No," Eric cleared his throat. "I'm not locking you in."

"Oh, hell," Connor muttered, "is she using mind control on him?"

He tossed a glare over his shoulder. "Ella isn't the enemy. Reece came after her. He's made her life hell. She deserves to see him brought to justice." His hand caught hers and he squeezed her fingers. "We've got a deal on that."

Then he pulled her to his side as they faced off against the other two. If Shane or Connor had a problem with Ella, that would just be too bad.

He was sure his expression told them that very important fact.

Say the wrong thing, and we'll fight right here.

Shane was studying Ella with narrowed eyes. Was there the faintest hint of recognition in his stare? Shane *had* been there the night Ella was pulled from the basement, but there'd been so much chaos then that Eric didn't think the two had even shared more than a fast glance.

"What about the wings?" Connor wanted to know. "Don't you think we all deserve an explanation on that?"

Okay, so he should have asked about them. But he'd been busy building her trust.

Bullshit. An internal voice called him on that. He'd just been busy getting lost in her.

"My wings?" Ella's body brushed against Eric's. "He knows all about those."

Actually, he didn't. He had a few suspicions. A few rumors and myths that he'd picked up over the years, but Eric had no proof. Not that he'd admit that right then. Long ago, he'd learned to always act as if he knew what the hell was happening.

Even when he didn't necessarily.

The fact that the wings had vanished back inside her body—and not left any external sign—that sure hinted that he was dealing with a shifter. Had it only been a partial shift? That was his suspicion. Connor's mate Chloe had only been able to partially shift into a wolf form. She'd never managed to fully become the beast. Maybe Ella was like that, too.

He opened his mouth to speak—

But Ella gave a little gasp and she stepped toward Shane. "I know you." Her hand reached out, as if she'd touch him. "I just saw you in my dream."

Oh, the hell, no. Before she could touch the vampire, Eric caught her hand and pulled her back to his side. Then he kept his arm around her shoulders for good measure. She did not need to be touching Shane. For any reason.

Jealousy. Is this what it feels like? Burning, twisting, making his fangs ache. This shit was *not* good.

And why the hell had she been dreaming about Shane?

"A field of blood and sand," Ella said quietly. "With death all around."

Eric's shoulders stiffened as he shot a fast glance at Shane. Ella should *not* know about that. Very few did.

During a battle, on a mission that had gone to hell and back, life had changed for Eric.

He'd died.

Then been brought back.

"Uh, yeah..." Connor rubbed his jaw. "There's obviously a lot going on here, but how about we handle one issue at a time. I've got one seriously beat-up werewolf downstairs and the guy is begging to tell you all he knows about Keegan James. So how about we handle him and then figure out what's up with the winged vampiress here? I mean, if she's on our team now, great. The more, the merrier, but I personally want to find out where the hell Keegan is right now. Because I'd *thought* he'd burned in that fire and if that SOB is still out there and he might come after my Chloe again..." His nails turned into claws. "I need to make sure that *doesn't* happen."

Connor was an alpha werewolf. And a vampire. A deadly mix that most thought couldn't be created.

Until recently, it hadn't been possible. But Eric had personally overseen the development of the cross-overs.

The Para Unit was changing the world. Or maybe, the world was just evolving again.

With a little help from the monsters, magic, and good old science.

***

For once, she wasn't the one being watched. It was a rather novel experience for Ella. She stood in the observation room, her hands hovering near the cold glass, as she stared into the interrogation room. The werewolf who'd called himself Reece was already in there.

And even with his werewolf healing powers, the guy looked like hell.

"Shouldn't he be…not so bruised? Not so bloody?" Ella finally asked as she slanted a quick glance at Connor.

Eric had sent her and Connor into observation. He and the other guy—the man who'd appeared in her dreams, Shane—were about to enter the interrogation room.

"The silver limits his healing," Connor told her. "The guy was injected with…a lot…of silver earlier."

Her gaze slid back to Reece. "He wanted to kidnap me again. Probably starve me, take all my blood, and then dump my body somewhere." It was hard to feel much sympathy for him. "He was there the first time I was taken, too." Her hand pressed against the glass. "He was laughing that night. I've never been able to forget his laughter."

"He's not laughing now," Connor told her grimly.

No, he wasn't.

The door to the interrogation room opened. Shane and Eric headed inside. As soon as he saw Eric, Reece tensed and fear flashed on his face.

"The other werewolves sure did a number on him," Ella said.

There was a stark pause beside her. Then Connor asked, "What made you think it was the others?"

"Well, I figured they assumed he'd talk—he *is* about to talk and—"

"Eric gave him those marks."

She shook her head.

"I don't think he liked it when the guy in there told him that the big master plan was to cut your wings off."

Ice slid over her skin. "Eric attacked him."

"In fairness, Reece did challenge the guy. Some stupid one-on-one crap. Only you don't really ever want to go one-on-one with Eric Pate."

"No," her voice had gone hoarse. "You don't."

"I think the big boss is letting this case get too personal."

Her gaze was on the men in that interrogation room. Only they weren't really men. So much more.

"And that's all because of you," Connor said.

***

Keegan had followed the SUVs to the base. Tricky Para Agents—hiding in plain sight. The warehouse truly looked like nothing from the outside.

He'd bet the damn thing probably went down past the ground for several floors. A whole hidden base, right there.

The agents he'd trailed slipped past security after they flashed their IDs. He wasn't going to have that easy get-in option. No one would just wave him inside and let him go.

So he'd just fight his way in there. Fight and kill because he had nothing left to lose.

Either I get Ella or I die.

He took a step forward.

There was a rustle then, a sweep of wind that went around him. He tensed and glanced at the darkness surrounding him. Dawn was close, but the shadows around the building were still too thick and heavy.

His eyes narrowed as he tried to see through those shadows. His vision wasn't nearly as strong as it had been *before* he'd burned a dozen times, but…someone was out there. Something.

Waiting.

His lips curled in a smile. Maybe he wasn't the only one in the mood to storm the Para Unit's stronghold.

Good. Maybe someone else could help him with this particular bit of dirty work.

"Let's play," Keegan murmured. Then he rushed forward, moving toward the guard station. The guy whirled toward him.

Keegan shoved a knife in the man's stomach.

***

"So Keegan's not dead..." Reece's shoulders lifted and fell in a rough shrug. "You knew that shit, though, right?"

Eric braced his legs and kept his hands loose at his sides. He stared down at Reece, aware of Shane circling to stand behind the guy. The better to prepare for any attack that might be coming. "Yes, I knew that shit." He inclined his head toward Reece. "I want to know where he is."

"Canada. Went across the border to be safe." Reece was talking fast now. "I'm gonna want transport out of here. Those other damn wolves already think I turned—*because of you!*"

"Um, you *are* turning on them," Eric pointed out.

Spittle flew from Reece's mouth. "'Cause you gave me no choice! I was just following orders! Hell, what does one freaking fey matter, anyway? She's the last one, then—poof, all gone."

Fey. Eric's heartbeat quickened, but he didn't change expression. "You want transport, you want safety, then you keep talking to me."

"Keegan is hurt. Bad. He survived that fire." Reece whistled. "I don't even know how the hell he did that. He burned over and over and kept healing—must have been her blood. It's the only thing that makes sense. But he's weak now. Nearly human."

Stop underestimating humans. They weren't nearly as weak as jerks like Reece liked to believe.

"He said we had to bring her in. That she could make him strong again. The wings are supposed to work, you see. They create life, give power. That's where we all came from, if you believe that shit—from the wings. Some mad scientist got hold of them and started playing God," he muttered. "Stories…"

Eric glanced toward the observation glass. His own reflection stared back at him, but he knew Ella was in there. He could feel her.

Did I really drink her blood? He'd always tried to be so careful. But with her, he'd lost all thought of restraint. Even at that moment, he wanted to taste her again. Again and again, endlessly.

"How did Keegan know Ella would be at that bar?" Eric asked, his jaw locking.

"Her kind…never walks away. Revenge is in their blood." Reece cast a nervous glance toward the mirror. He leaned forward, as if he were about to impart some big secret to Eric and he said, "That's why they were the first experiments. Too dangerous. Too evil. I think that fool who got hold of them…he thought he could make something better." Reece laughed. "But he just made us instead. More monsters in the world…"

***

"That laughter," Ella said as she wrapped her arms around her stomach. "How could I forget it? How could I walk away? It wasn't going to happen. Not for me. Not after what they did. They treated me like an animal. Worse..."

"And you went to kill them."

"It's my way." Even to her own ears, her voice sounded sad. "That wasn't fixed despite what that fool thought." *Fool*...Reese's word. She'd called the man many things—sick, twisted.

Lover.

Enemy.

"Um," Connor cleared his throat, "and the fool would be?"

Her laughter came again. "Surely you realize that some myths...some old stories are a little bit true. Like Frankenstein...Cedric wanted to play God. It's not as if he's the first guy to do that."

"Are you telling me Frankenstein is real?"

Ella smiled at the shock in his tone and peered over at him. "No. I'm saying that there have been men over time who thought they could make bigger, better monsters."

His eyelids flickered. "Yeah, I know about those men. Met a few like that."

She looked back through the glass. "I thought I was the last of my kind. Until Eric."

Connor swore.

Her gaze cut to him once more.

"Sorry," he muttered.

Like she cared about his curses.

"You think Eric Pate…is like you?" Connor asked her carefully.

She shook her head. "Not *just* like me. He's my mate." There would be no more denying what her instincts were telling her.

Connor rocked back on his heels. "Okay, yeah, I get that the two of you had sex earlier. He was practically growling when he opened the door, but sex *isn't* mating. Surely you know that."

"I know that." Her cheeks burned. She didn't need to be told that by this guy. "I also know the connection that I feel with my kind. I can *only* mate with another like me." For an instant, tears stung her eyes. "Do you know what it's like to think you're the only one of your kind for centuries? To be so totally alone? When Keegan had me and the days and nights swam together, I started to wonder…what was the point? Why was I fighting so hard? Nothing was waiting for me out there. No one…" She smiled. "But I was wrong. Eric was out there. All along. I just didn't know it."

"Oh, fuck," Connor said. "This is bad."

"No, it's good." Why wasn't he getting that?

***

Getting inside that big gate was actually much easier than Keegan had anticipated. The

Para Agents were far too arrogant. So very certain of their secret location.

All he had to do was kill the three guards at the front entrance. Then he stripped one guard and took his clothes and ID. That ID gave him instant access to the base. Keegan took his silver loaded guns and he just waltzed toward the main entrance. Easy as can be…

The rustle of sound reached his ears once again. A flutter. Almost like wings, right above him. His head whipped back.

But nothing was there.

Nothing.

He swiped the guard's ID over the security access screen. The control panel flashed green, and those big doors began to open…

Wind blew against him. Fierce, strong…

He whirled around just as the beast flew out of the shadows. Big and strong and—

Claws sank into Keegan's chest. He fired the silver bullets into the bastard. Again and again and again.

The beast before him just laughed.

Then he grabbed Keegan and flew straight up into the air. *"I know what you've done…"* That voice was so low and sinister and the creature's wings were beating all around Keegan. He tried to fight but—

There were no more bullets left.

"Where is she?"

"Inside!" Keegan yelled, knowing there could only be one person the creature sought. "She's—"

An alarm was sounding. Loud and shrieking.

And Keegan was suddenly—falling.

***

When he heard the shriek of the alarm, Eric immediately ran for the door. He rushed out of the interrogation room even as he roared for other agents to guard Reece. He and Shane didn't wait for the elevator—they just ran for the exterior of the base, rushing up the stairs as fast as they could.

Eric paused only long enough to grab his gun and then he was running outside with other agents.

And he found a dead man on the ground.

Less than five feet from the entrance to the base, a man's body sprawled across the pavement. His neck was twisted at an unnatural angle, his legs and arms bent…and there was so much blood.

"What in the hell…" Shane exclaimed. "What happened to him? What *did* that?"

Eric bent near the body. He couldn't see the fellow's face yet. It had to be one of his own agents, judging by the uniform. "I need teams to sweep the area." His hand touched the guy's throat. No pulse. He hadn't expected one, but he'd still needed to check. Dammit. He *hated* losing men. His agents were good people. They were trying to protect others. They…

His hand brushed over the side of the dead man's head. He saw the red, raised skin. Burn marks.

Not my agent.

Eric sucked in a sharp breath as he turned the fellow's head. Smashed and sickening because the guy had apparently hit the ground face-first but…

"Keegan?" Eric could still make out the guy's features. And those burns—burns that he could now see on the man's neck, on half of his face, and on his hands—those burns were a dead giveaway.

Sonofabitch. The guy on the ground was Keegan. In one of the Para Agent's uniforms.

"Check the area!" Eric roared. "There could be more—"

"Three men down," Lawrence said as he ran toward Eric, his chest heaving. "Shot, and one of the agents had been stripped."

No, no, *no.* "You were coming inside, weren't you?" Eric snarled to the dead man. "You thought you'd get her." He could even see the keycard now, tossed a few feet away from Keegan's body. The man had been ready to waltz right inside the base.

There was a sharp gasp, and Eric glanced over to see that Ella had pushed her way through the crowd of agents. She stood there, with her hand over her mouth. Looking terrified. Shocked.

Connor hurried past her and came to Eric's side. "Boss…" Connor's voice was low. "His injuries…that guy was *dropped* from a damn high height. And right now, I only know one person around here with wings who could lift up a guy like that and drop him."

And Eric was staring straight at her.

"But she was with me," Connor added. "I swear she was. She didn't do this."

Agents were swarming the area.

Wind blew against Eric's face.

He heard the faintest rustle, almost like leaves blowing nearby.

"Take Ella back inside," he ordered immediately.

"It's Keegan," she said and she rushed forward, her eyes so wide. "It's him!"

The man who'd kidnapped her. Tortured her.

Eric's arm wrapped around her stomach, pulling her away from the dead man. "I need you to go inside the base," he whispered into her ear. "Sweetheart, listen to me. It isn't safe. You have to go back inside."

Keegan had planned to slip into the base and attack.

Something had stopped him.

Something that was still there…Still waiting? *Someone.*

Ella nodded. "Okay…" But she sounded almost lost and despite the power he knew she held, Ella felt fragile in his arms. She nodded once more and then slowly backed away. His gaze cut to Connor and the guy immediately moved toward her.

Ella took a few tentative steps back toward the base—

"What the fuck…" Lawrence called out, voice shocked. He jerked his gun up and aimed at the sky. "Incoming!"

Eric lifted his own weapon because sure-as-hell enough, something was coming at them from the sky. The wingspan on the thing had to be at least ten feet. Its wings were heavy and black, and it was hurtling right toward them.

No, toward Ella…

"Stay away from her!" Eric yelled and he opened fire.

But the man up there—and, yeah, he could see the body of a man—just dodged the bullets in lightning fast moves.

"Tranq him!" Eric ordered his men. "Take him out!" Eric lunged for Ella.

She was just standing there, staring with wide eyes and parted lips as she gazed up at the being hurtling toward her. Faster, faster, the guy was closing in on her.

If he touches her, he'll take her from me.

Eric reached out for her. His fingers tangled with hers.

White-hot pain ripped across his back. Eric locked his teeth and tackled Ella, sending them both hurtling to the pavement even as his men unleashed a maelstrom of gunfire on the winged SOB.

His back burned—no, not burned. *Bled.* He could feel his blood soaking his shirt. But Ella was all right. She hadn't been taken. *She was all right.*

He lifted his head. She stared at him with a gaze full of shock. Her pupils were tiny pinpricks. "There can't be two of you," she said.

Eric was nothing like that winged bastard.

He looked over his shoulder. His agents were giving him cover fire. He knew they'd hit the assailant, but the guy hadn't fallen. He was up in the air right then, no doubt getting ready for another swipe at them. *Another attempt to take her.*

Eric picked Ella up into his arms and ran toward the doors of the base. Wind whipped around him and he held her more tightly than he'd ever held anything before. His feet thundered over the pavement. Fast. Fast.

Fast.

They cleared the doors. Gunfire rang out.

And a roar filled the night.

CHAPTER EIGHT

"You're hurt."

The doors had sealed behind them, and Eric had gone completely still. Ella twisted in his arms, trying to get free because she could smell his blood. He'd been attacked, while trying to shield her.

Why would one of my own kind want to hurt me?

But the guy had. He'd been dive-bombing right toward her.

Eric didn't let her go. He just tightened his hold on her, using that powerful strength that she usually found to be a turn-on, just not right then because she was too worried about him.

"Eric!"

He surged forward, moving quickly through the winding labyrinth that was the base. His hold never wavered on her, but the scent of his blood grew stronger, scaring her.

Then he rounded a corner and headed into another room. One glance inside and she knew it was a medical ward. She could see the exam tables. The surgical equipment. Bandages.

He carefully put her down on one of the exam tables.

"I'm not the one who got hurt!" She hopped right off that table and pushed him around so that she could see his back. "You were the one who—*Eric.*" He'd been hurt so much worse than she realized. Long claw marks slid over his back, cutting deeply into his skin, digging into muscle and…*bone?* Blood seeped from his wounds. Such terrible, terrible wounds.

How was he even standing? Much less carrying her all around the place.

She turned her head to the side, immediately offering her neck to him. "Drink."

His hands curled around her shoulders. Did he stagger a bit? Ella thought he had.

"You don't…" Eric rasped, "Need to give me…"

Ella shook her head. "I will give you everything that I have." Didn't he get that? Once, long ago, that was how she'd been raised. Always taught that she'd find a mate who was her match and that they would bond, forever. "Drink, Eric, please." Tears stung her eyes because she hated to see him in pain.

He leaned over her. His breath blew against her neck. Then his teeth sank into her. Pleasure rolled through her—she thought it always would with him—but she tried to push it away. This was about him. Only him. He needed to drink so he'd heal.

Fear was a knot in her belly. She didn't want anything to happen to Eric. Not when she'd just found him. Fate couldn't be cruel enough to do this to her now.

Her hands curled around him. Carefully, though, so she wouldn't touch his wounds. "He must have been trying to take your wings," she said. "Even our own kind…the stories used to circulate that if you cut deep enough, you might find the wings."

He tensed. His tongue slid over her skin, and then she felt the light touch of his lips. Kissing her. "He wasn't going for my wings." His voice was stronger. Good. So good. "He was going for you." Eric eased back and stared down at her.

His color was better. He'd been nearly ashen before but now his normal golden tone had returned. Her Eric seemed to be coming back.

"Did you know him?" Eric asked her.

Ella shook her head. "He moved so fast." She swallowed. "It doesn't make sense. I-I thought we were the only ones left…"

Something flickered in his gaze. "Ella—"

"*Eric!*" At that sharp cry, they both turned. She saw Connor standing in the doorway. Shane was right behind him. "Man, we followed your blood trail in here." Connor ran toward him. "What can I do? How can I—" He broke off and his gaze sharpened. "You sure look pretty good for a guy who bled out all around this facility."

Eric's lips pressed together.

"I gave him my blood," Ella said.

Connor and Shane shared a look. She didn't really like that look. It held too many secrets.

"Did you now…?" Shane said.

"Yes, I did." Hadn't she just said that? "And I'd do it again. He needed me."

Shane clamped a hand on Eric's shoulder. "Show us the damage."

Slowly, Eric turned.

Her breath heaved out in a relieved sigh. The wounds had already closed so much. "He won't get your wings," she said.

"Right," Connor drawled. "No one's taking your wings, Eric. I guess you're safe there."

Eric turned back around and glared at him. "Tell me that guy is in containment right now."

"I wish I could, but he got away. He was hit at least a dozen times, but there was no stopping him. If anything, the hits just seemed to make him stronger."

Ella frowned at them. "Of course, rage always fuels our kind."

"The fey," Shane said, his voice completely devoid of expression.

Ella nodded. "It would have just made him stronger."

"We need a gold net," Eric said.

At those words, Ella stepped back from him.

His hand flew out and caught hers. "He attacked us. We have to stop him."

She nodded, more slowly this time. "I-I know. Right. I—"

"I want you to head back to our apartment, Ella. I have to secure the base. I need the guards to be aware of just what they're dealing with."

She didn't want to leave him.

He leaned toward her. With his lips near her ear, he whispered, "I swear, I won't lock you in. I just need to know that you're safe. *Please,* do this for me."

Ella hesitated, but… "Okay."

He squeezed her fingers. "I'll have some guards take you there." He let her go and hurried toward the door. He called out and two men in black rushed inside.

She hesitated a moment, worried. "Is there something you aren't telling me?" Ella asked. She could practically feel the secrets in that room.

"No," Eric said immediately.

She smiled for him even as she felt the blow straight to her heart. "I'd really rather you not lie to me," Ella said as she turned away. "Because I won't be lying to you."

***

Eric watched her leave. Her words had made his chest ache. And, hell, wasn't he already in enough pain? But Ella—she'd looked so sad when he'd lied to her. He'd almost called her back and apologized. Explained.

And I never do that shit.

How screwed up was that? But Ella, she was different. The way he felt with her was different.

Her footsteps faded away.

"Dude," Connor finally said, "you are playing one dangerous game."

"I'm not playing any kind of game." He yanked off his shirt, ignoring the sting when the bloody garment tried to stick in his wounds.

"She thinks you're her mate," Connor told him. "Did you tell her that crap?"

Mate. His hands fisted around the bloody shirt. "No. I didn't." *I just had sex with her. Crazy, mind-blowing sex. And, yeah, maybe I feel like the woman took a bit of my battered soul.*

But…mated?

No, he wasn't a wolf. He didn't have any kind of biological connection with her, no primal DNA response. Mating was for werewolves. And, apparently, fey.

"Well, she sure thinks you are." Connor yanked a hand through his hair. "She thinks you're just like her."

"Fey," Shane added.

Why did the guy keep throwing that one particular word around?

"I don't even know what that is," Connor said as he began to pace. "Fey—that's fairies? Am I seriously dealing with fairies now?"

Shane shrugged. "It would explain the wings."

Connor paced faster. "Since when do fairies get fueled by rage?"

Eric understood that he had to share what he knew. Connor and Shane were two men he trusted the most. "They're only good in the movies. In the cartoons where they all sing and dance and grant wishes and shit." He rolled back his shoulders, feeling the faint pull of healing muscles in his back. *That prick is going to pay for what he did to me.* "If you look at real folklore, you'll see a different story."

"In plenty of old legends I grew up with…" Shane said slowly, "The fairies were wicked. The last thing you wanted to do was get on their bad side. They never forgave and they sure never forgot."

"*Stories,*" Connor fired. "Just—"

"Once people thought tales of men turning into wolves who howled in the night…those were just stories, too." Eric pointed out. "Now I guess we know better." He dropped his bloody shirt into a garbage bag. "Some Fey stories say that the women like to seduce mortal men. They make them into slaves…"

Did she seduce me?

Did I seduce her?

Does it fucking matter?

He cleared his throat. "Other tales say they like to kill…like to drown their victims. Like to lure prey to their deaths. They get some kind of power rush from that." He considered the bits and pieces of myth that he knew. "The sirens from Greek mythology—they were supposed to be fairies. They lived only for destruction." *That isn't Ella. She isn't like that.*

Connor stopped pacing. "You know more about her than you're saying."

"I suspected…the first time I saw her wings. There aren't a lot of creatures with wings like that. I was guessing she wasn't an angel…"

Connor's eyes doubled. "Holy shit. Are you saying *they're* out in the world, too?"

"I haven't seen them." *Doesn't mean they aren't flying around.* "But she had vampire fangs. The fangs didn't strike me as overly angelic." His lips twisted. "So I started to think she might be like you, Connor."

He saw understanding fill Connor's eyes just before his friend said, "A cross-over."

In Connor's case, the guy was half-vampire, half-werewolf. But for Ella…"Half-Fey, half-vampire." A combination he wouldn't have thought possible, not until he met her.

Connor snapped his fingers. "The freaking mad scientist."

Now Eric was the one who felt lost. "What?"

"When you were interrogating Reece, Ella and I started talking about *Frankenstein*."

Eric shot a quick glance at Shane. The vampire gave him an I-Have-No-Clue look in response.

Connor growled. "She said there was a mad scientist who tried to make monsters…kind of like the shit that the Para Unit does now. I think she said his name was Cedric."

Eric's spine snapped up. The healing skin pulled.

"Maybe she was made," Connor said, speaking quickly now. "And that's how she's a mix of-of Fey and vampire."

Maybe.

"It's not like you're the first one to play God with the monsters," Shane said.

Eric forced his jaw to unclench. The first monster he'd made…it had been himself. And even Shane didn't know exactly what he'd done.

"I got the impression," Connor continued, his voice hardening, "that she wasn't real keen on the mad scientist."

Shane whistled. "Not everyone enjoys being experimented on."

No. Eric squeezed his eyes shut as he tried to figure out what the hell he should do next. It would have been so much easier if he'd been able to keep his hands off Ella, but that hadn't been a possibility. He'd wanted her too much. *Still* wanted her too much. But when she found out…

"Shit," Connor said. "You're worried she's going to realize you're not her mate after all."

Eric's eyes snapped open. "Mating is all about biology. One being's ability to recognize a breeding partner on a strong, sexual level. A basic level. It's not some predestined souls connecting crap—"

"I wouldn't let your winged vampiress hear you say that," Connor cut through Eric's words. "Not if her temper is really as bad as we're suspecting. Who knows what else she can do if she gets mad enough?"

And that was the problem. He didn't know. None of them knew. *You didn't push her to learn the truth because you wanted her. Now all bets are off. The team has to understand the threat they are facing.*

"What do you think she'll do," Shane asked, "when she realizes you aren't just like her?"

"Better question," Connor added before Eric could reply—and he had no idea what he would have said, anyway. "*Why,*" Connor said, "does she even think you are like her? I mean, I've seen your fangs flash lately, so I get the vampire part.

But you don't seem like some rage-fueled creature to me."

Because he controlled his rage. He never let his beast out. *Never.* Eric glanced between Shane and Connor. "Steps had to be taken," he said gruffly. "I needed to make sure I would be strong enough to handle the threats that would come my way."

Connor's eyelids flickered. "What did you do to yourself?"

"I didn't always have a choice. I've been bitten by vampires and werewolves. I had to see what would happen with the bites, *before* I exposed any of my men to those threats. And after the bites, someone had to be the test subject for the drugs that the Para Unit created—someone had to make sure they didn't cause death or insanity." He'd been that someone. "I wasn't going to put others at risk."

"Are you a cross-over?" Connor finally asked him.

A cross-over. A werewolf who'd been bitten by a vampire—an alpha werewolf who'd survived that blood exchange to become something more. "No, I'm one hell of a lot worse."

He was the monster that had been created in labs. Made not just with magic but science. And that was why he suspected Ella was so confused about him. His altered genetics were throwing her off. She thought he was something that he wasn't.

And I deliberately let her keep thinking that way.

"She is going to be so pissed," Connor said, seeming to follow Eric's thoughts completely.

"We need to bring in an expert," Eric said. He turned to Shane. "Olivia is the best at this. Can you get her ready for a sit-down with Ella?" Dr. Olivia Maddox was an expert when it came to understanding the minds of paranormal creatures. She was also the woman Shane loved. The woman that the vampire had once been willing to kill for. *And I bet he'd kill for her again, in an instant.*

Shane hesitated. "I'll get her ready, but only if you promise that your Ella won't go into some rage frenzy and attack Olivia. Because that *won't* happen."

"No, it won't." He'd see to it. Eric exhaled on a long sigh. "We'll get gold collars and cuffs ready, just in case." Even as he said those words, his stomach clenched. The last thing he wanted to do was imprison Ella.

No, actually, the last thing he wanted was to hurt her.

Too late. When the truth about me comes out, she'll be plenty hurt.

***

She'd waited in the apartment for nearly an hour. During that whole time, Ella had paced, practically wearing a hole in the carpet.

He was like me. He was like me. The man who'd come flying toward her had been another of her kind. His black wings had stretched so far.

What were the odds? After all of this time, she'd found not one, but *two* others who were like her.

Amazing.

Terrifying.

The door opened. She spun around and when she saw Eric standing there, Ella ran toward him. She threw her arms around him and just held on tight.

A bit slowly, hesitantly, his hands lifted and curled around her shoulders.

Immediately, her fear began to subside. "I don't like for you to be hurt," Ella said.

His hold tightened on her. "And I never want you hurt."

That was nice. They were definitely making progress. Ella eased back and stared up at him. "You weren't able to track him, were you?"

Eric shook his head. "He was too fast for us." His hand slid toward her cheek and he brushed back a lock of her hair. "You know, he was trying to take you."

Ella nodded. *Take me, hurt you.*

"You didn't recognize him?"

"I didn't get a chance to see his face. I just saw his wings." Wings...*like mine.*

"There's someone I want you to talk with," Eric said quietly.

She tensed. "Not another doctor. I *hate* all of those tests." Not that Holly wasn't nice and all but...*enough.*

"Olivia Maddox is a different kind of doctor. One who specializes in understanding people like us."

Ella tilted her head back to study him.

"I need insight on this guy. By talking to her, you'll help me figure things out."

A smile curved her lips. "I want to help you."

"I know." He dropped his hands and backed away from her. "Olivia is waiting for us now. We should go."

He'd put on a new t-shirt. She couldn't see his wounds, but when he turned away, her hand reached out and lightly touched his shoulder. "Are you better now?"

He stilled. "Yes."

"I'm so glad." Because she'd been terrified. Eric shouldn't hurt like that. No one should ever try to kill him.

Or take his wings.

Eric cleared his throat. "Come on. We need to go."

She followed him and a few moments later, they were in the elevator. She noticed that he was keeping a very careful distance between them. Alarm bells began to go off in Ella's head, and, deliberately, she reached out, twining her fingers with his.

At first, she thought he'd pull away from her. Instead, Eric's fingers tightened around hers. Then he lifted her hand and pressed a kiss to her knuckles, right before the elevator doors slid open.

They were on a new floor. A higher floor. Agents bustled around the hallway. And a woman with black hair, wearing an elegant suit stood a few feet away, just watching them. There was something about her stare—it was a little too intense, and Ella had the uncomfortable feeling that woman could see right through her.

Then the woman smiled. It was a friendly, open smile. It should have reassured Ella. It didn't.

The lady stepped forward, offering her hand. "Hello, my name is Olivia, and I'm here to help you."

At those words, Ella stiffened. "I didn't realize I needed help." But she took the offered hand, shook it quickly, then immediately let go.

"We can all use some help," the woman said. Her black hair was secured in some kind of twist. She motioned toward the hallway. "Why don't you come with me?"

Ella had left the elevator, but now she hesitated. Her gaze turned to Eric. "What's going on?"

"Olivia needs to ask you some questions."

This wasn't right. Ella licked her lips and said, "If *you* have questions, Eric. Ask them. Don't you think you can trust my answers?"

His mouth tightened. "This is Olivia's area of expertise." Then he backed away. "I have to check in with my team. I'll be back to collect you shortly."

Collect you. "You collect things," she said as he stepped into the elevator. "Not people."

His gaze flickered.

The doors shut.

Olivia cleared her throat. "Shall we get started?"

Ella rolled back her shoulders. "At least you aren't the kind of doctor that likes to cut me open and see what makes me tick." She headed to Olivia's side. Together, they walked down the hallway. Their steps were oddly in sync. "I'm guessing you're just the kind that peeks into my head and tries to find all of the secrets that I have."

Olivia stopped near an unmarked door on the right. "I've helped a lot of your kind."

Ella had to laugh at those particular words. "Trust me, you haven't. I don't think you know anything about *my* kind." But she went into the room. No exam tables were inside. Just comfy chairs. A desk. Even a couch. Classic shrink set-up. "I guess the doctor will see me now," Ella murmured.

The door shut behind her with a soft click. "It's all right, Ella. This is a safe place for you. It's just us—"

But Ella laughed. "You think I don't know when he's watching?" She'd already spotted the tiny camera in the upper left side of the room. "He's always watching." Goosebumps rose on her arms.

Olivia's gaze shot toward the camera. Her eyes widened with what looked like shock. As if Ella would buy that. She shook her head and got comfy on the couch. She could play mind games with the best of them.

Only…

She wasn't really in the mood to play games any longer. "Let's just get this over with…"

***

Eric booted up his computer and a few taps on his keyboard had the feed to Olivia's office immediately opening on his screen. Olivia would be pissed when she found out about the camera. She always wanted total privacy when she dealt with her paranormal patients, but if Olivia's little side trip to Purgatory had taught them anything…it was that the paranormals couldn't be trusted. Olivia had been attacked when she went in to help the paranormals in Purgatory.

The camera was a security measure that had to be utilized. For Olivia's safety.

Even if the patient was Ella.

Ella was on the couch now, stretching out. She appeared totally relaxed, a bit surprising to him. He'd thought she'd completely rebel when she saw Olivia and fully realized just what was happening. When he'd had her in containment before, he'd considered sending Olivia in, but he'd hesitated. *I wanted her stronger first.*

She was plenty strong now. Hopefully, she'd face the demons in her past and Olivia would get Ella to talk all about those demons. *So I can learn how to fight them.*

Questioning Ella directly wasn't an option. Ella just looked at him with that sexy gaze of hers, and he wanted to hold her. Screw her secrets. And as the director of the Para Unit, he couldn't have the luxury of overlooking Ella's past—and her secrets just might be a matter of national security.

What the fuck is wrong with me? When did I lose all objectivity?

A knock sounded at his door. The door opened before he could say anything and his sister Holly marched inside. "You've been *drinking* from her?" she demanded.

Trust Holly to learn his secrets. Had Connor been the one to rat him out to her? Probably.

At least she'd shut the door before her big announcement. He waved her closer and looked back at the scene. "I don't really have time for this now," he said, "look, I've got—"

Her hands slammed down on the desk. "You make time."

His brows lifted as he glanced over at her.

There were tears gleaming in Holly's eyes. "You make time. You listen to me." Her breath heaved out. "I've been doing more tests on the blood we took from her. Her blood…it's not like any normal vampire blood I've ever seen. You know we always thought that vampirism was a virus—"

"Spread and activated through the blood exchange. Yes, I know," he said carefully. The virus only activated if the human prey was at the brink of death during the exchange. The human had to both *give* the vampire blood and *take* the vampire's blood. And death had to be seconds away. So close. Then the body entered its final moments and fought ferociously for life, and during that fight, the virus activated.

He and Holly had been working to try and find a cure for the virus, only he'd pretty much given up hope of ever finding that cure. He'd adjusted. He'd become something…else.

"I mixed her blood with regular vampire blood," Holly said, swallowing. "I studied the results to see what would happen..."

He stood up.

"Her blood took over the cells. It—it just...*annihilated* them. There was no transformation. There was just destruction. Her blood isn't some kind of secret to a cure, if that's what you were hoping."

No, no, he hadn't—

"I think her blood can *kill* vampires." Her lower lip trembled. "And if you've been drinking it like Connor said..."

He *had* sold Eric out.

"Then I need you in my lab immediately. I have to do blood work on you. I have to make sure that she hasn't killed you." Her breath heaved out. "Because you could be dying right now and not know it. Her blood could be killing you as we speak!"

Eric sagged back against the chair. "That's not possible."

But Holly flew around the desk and came to his side. Her hand grabbed his wrist and held on tight. "It is possible! I ran the tests a dozen times. Her blood is *lethal* to vampires, and if you've been taking it, you could die." She tightened her hold on him. "I can't let that happen. You protected me. You made me live, and I'm going to make absolutely certain that you do, too."

Eric shook his head. Holly didn't understand. His gaze slid back to the monitor. To Ella.

A lethal package to wipe out vampires? "She transformed Keegan. Gave him her blood—"

"He was an alpha werewolf, not a vampire. So he had a different reaction to her. That's probably why he was walking around like the living dead, covered in burns when he should have been on his way to hell."

His gaze slid to her. "Connor sure has been talking to you a lot."

"Your agents brought the body to me. He *should* have been killed in that fire, but something kept him alive. That something—it's her blood." Now her eyes slid to the screen even as she kept her hold on Eric. "She's dangerous, Eric. A complete unknown. And I don't…I don't usually say this, you know I don't, but…for everyone's safety…" Her voice dropped to a whisper. "I think she needs to be contained."

CHAPTER NINE

"When were you born, Ella?"

Ella stared up at the ceiling. "A very, very long time ago."

"You were born a vampire? Or you became one?"

Ah, well, at least the lady wasn't beating around the bush. "I don't understand why Eric didn't just ask me these questions. I mean, we have a deal. It's not like I'd lie to him."

Silence. Was she supposed to be uncomfortable with silence? Was it supposed to make her talk? She knew that silence was a tactic some shrinks used. "Silence doesn't work on me," Ella said. "I started to like it when I was in Keegan's basement." Actually, she'd grown used to silence centuries before Keegan had come into her life. *Another time, another prison…*

Olivia was seated in the chair near her. She wasn't writing down notes or tapping away on a laptop. She just seemed to be listening.

How good for her.

"Do you want to talk about the time in his basement?"

Ella kept staring at the ceiling. Were they on the first floor? They'd gone up on the elevator, so she thought so. There were windows to the right—windows currently covered by some seriously thick blinds. "Talk about it? Not really. I don't want to even think about the time in the basement. It was hell, but it's over. I'm out."

"And now Keegan is dead."

Ella turned her head and met Olivia's stare. "Yes." She'd seen his body with her own eyes. He wouldn't be torturing her ever again.

"According to accounts..." Olivia's voice and face both held no expression. "A man with black wings killed him. He took Keegan up high—"

"And then dropped him," Ella said. "So Keegan knew what was happening when he fell. He had time to fear. In those last few seconds as he plummeted, he knew he would die...so he had to wonder what the next life would be like for him. A fire that never ended. Torment or just...nothing at all. Darkness." Darkness...like the dark basement he'd kept her in. Day and night. So many days. So many nights and—

"You wanted him to die."

Ella laughed. "Really? Is it that obvious? I mean, I was only hunting the guy..."

"How do you feel knowing someone else took your prey?"

Her shoulders slid along the couch. Was that leather? Felt like it. The Para guys had sure gone all out with the shrink's pad. "I'm just relieved that I don't have to keep looking over my shoulder. Keegan won't be a threat to me any longer."

"You don't feel bad that he's dead?"

Feel—Ella turned her head and met the doctor's stare. "No," her words were flat. "I don't feel bad. I don't feel bad at all that the man who drugged me, who starved me, who *bled* me, is dead. I don't feel bad at all that the man who made my life a nightmare for *weeks* is gone. I don't feel bad about that even a little bit. I'm *relieved,*" she said again. "So if that makes me an evil person, if that makes me bad in your book, I don't really give a damn."

"Good and evil can be relative terms."

Ella laughed. "Right. And sometimes, they can be pretty clear cut." She was still staring into the shrink's eyes. "Tell me, Olivia," Ella murmured. "Do you ever wish that you could be someone else? Maybe some*thing* else?"

Olivia flinched. "I try not to wish at all."

"Really? Cause I wish all the time. I wish that Keegan hadn't taken me. I wish that I didn't have so much rage inside of me. I wish that I hadn't been *made* to be this way." She tried to swallow down some of the rage that was rising in her. Ella realized she'd clenched her hands into tight fists.

"Because, you see, I wasn't born like this, no. I was born differently. But another man, long ago, he thought he could make me better. A little *less* evil. He caught me. He made me his prisoner too, and then he started with *his* tests…"

***

Eric's chest seemed to burn as he heard Ella's words. "Go get your tool kit," he said to Holly. "Draw my blood. Run it through your machines. You'll see that she hasn't hurt me."

"You're too certain," Holly said. But, like him, her attention now seemed to be primarily on the nearby monitor. "Why are you so certain?"

"Because you don't know what I did *before* you joined the fold at the Para Unit. There were other doctors. Some *almost* as brilliant as you. I had to make sure I'd be strong enough to run this division. I had to be ready in case a werewolf attacked me or if another vampire came ready to bite." But one night, a vamp hadn't just gone after him. The vamp had tried to take out Holly.

Eric hadn't been ready to let his sister die. She'd transformed that night—and been introduced to his world.

Eric cleared his throat. "Go get your tools," he said again. "Test me, and you'll finally see the truth about me."

Her fingers fell away from his wrist. "Another mad scientist? We seem to be tripping over those guys these days."

"I wanted the changes," he said. "I went in with my eyes wide open." His breath sighed out and his hand lifted, almost touching the screen. "But she didn't."

The ache in his chest got worse.

***

"Who was this man?" Olivia asked.

"I loved him." She hadn't meant to say those words, had she? Maybe. Didn't matter. "I thought I did, anyway. I thought he loved me, too. But he didn't love me as I was. He-he wanted to change me. Because my *kind* was too dangerous. So he started his experiments. Not just on me, but on others like me. He took their wings." Her shoulders pressed back against the couch. Her wings were long gone now. They'd only come out if she had a rage-fueled shift. "And he used them to make other things."

The silence came again. But this time, Ella thought that silence might be from shock.

So she just waited.

The silence truly didn't bother her. The ghosts that used to scream at her were long gone.

Finally, Olivia whispered, "What things?"

"Werewolves." So sad and twisted—her ex-lover had created the very beings that had tried to destroy her. "You know, some humans have DNA that lets them change when they're bitten. They can transform, but it's such a small percentage of the population. So few." A fleeting smile curved her lips. "Have you ever wondered how the first human transformed into a werewolf? It was from the wings, you see. Our wings have so much power. Cut them off, grind them up, and they are very, very potent…my mad scientist injected a serum straight into a—a *volunteer's* bones. The change came then. So fast. And when you make one werewolf…well, it's only a matter of time until you have more."

She could hear the frantic pounding of Olivia's heartbeat. The faster rush of her breath. "You're saying…*you* created werewolves?"

Ella shook her head. Hadn't the woman been listening? Bad, for a shrink. "I'm saying others like me were killed. Our wings were taken and used to give birth to a whole new being—a werewolf."

"Why?"

"He didn't know werewolves would be born. I think he just wanted to see what would happen if he gave a human the serum. He had to experiment on someone else, first, of course, before he took the serum himself." Ella laughed. "It was just his bad luck that his *volunteer* turned out to be part of the human population with the altered DNA. But you just can't predict for some things like that."

Silence. Ella began to count in her mind. She'd just gotten to nineteen when—

"You don't say his name."

Ella pressed her lips together.

"You said he was your ex-lover and a mad scientist, but you won't say his name."

She wished there was something on the ceiling to focus upon. A crack. Spider webs. Something. Not just that perfect white space.

"Is it because if you say his name, you will remember him as a man and not as the monster you learned he was?"

Ella unclenched her fists and stared at her tiny claws. "I'm the monster."

"I don't think that's true."

Ella cut a quick glance her way. "That's because you haven't seen me when I'm at my worst. I hope you never do."

"Tell me his name, Ella."

She'd said it before, to Connor, and just uttering his name had left a bad taste in her mouth.

"Why are you afraid? It's just a name. It's just—"

"Cedric. Cedric Wallington." Now her heart was the one pounding too fast. "The human who tricked me. The human I let destroy my world. I had always been told to mate only with my own kind. That my *one* true partner was out there. To just wait…" Her breath heaved out. "But I didn't wait. I let him get to me, and everyone else paid the price."

Now her gaze slid to the camera. She stared up at that lens. "I'm sorry that I didn't wait. I'm so sorry all of the others died."

"Why are you apologizing? To him?"

At least Olivia wasn't pretending that Eric wasn't watching them. "Because Eric is like me. I thought we were all gone, but he's here. If I'd just found him sooner, if I'd just not given up hope of finding him—"

"Stop!"

Now she looked back at Olivia once more. Olivia's eyes were burning with fury. "Is that what Eric told you?" The shrink demanded. "That he's like you are?"

"No, he didn't say that but…" It was so hard to explain. "But I can sense it. I can feel it. When he bites me…it's just the way I was told it would be. The connection is there. Strong and powerful and—"

"Eric isn't like you."

Ella sat up and swung her legs to the side of the couch. "How do you know that?"

"I—" Olivia snapped her mouth closed and glared at the camera. After a moment, she nearly snarled, "*Get in here. Have you been lying to her?*

All this time? I won't do that to her, Eric! I won't lie!"

Ella's stomach was in knots. Eric hadn't lied to her. This woman was wrong. "I think I know my mate."

"Mating is biology. Genetics. Your body trying to trick your mind into thinking that you've found some kind of perfect half." Olivia waved her hands angrily. "That's how the future is guaranteed. Sex. Reproduction. Your body finds a good, potential match. It's not about souls or hearts or anything. It's science."

"Fine." Ella had followed her heart before, and it had taken her to death. "I'll take your science. My body recognizes him, it has from the beginning. He is meant for me. I know that. I—"

"I think he's using you," Olivia said. "I wish—"

Then her hands flew over her mouth.

Okay, the shrink was odd. Really odd.

Ella forced a rough laugh. "Unless you're a djinn, it's pretty safe to make wishes."

Olivia's eyes were the size of saucers.

Ella's gut twisted into knots. "You had better not be a djinn." Because one djinn had wrecked her world before.

Oliva's hands dropped away from her mouth. "Too late," she whispered. "I thought it."

So maybe Ella wasn't the one who should be getting a psychiatric chat. "You thought—what?"

"I wished you'd know the truth about Eric." Olivia had paled. "I'm sorry."

The scene just got weirder and weirder. But the woman seemed to be in such genuine distress that Ella reached out and curled her hand around the lady's shoulder. "It's okay. Wishes aren't bad things. They don't hurt anyone." *Unless you're a djinn. So for both of our sakes…*

Olivia's lashes slowly lifted. "Mine do."

"Tell me you aren't a djinn."

Olivia cleared her throat. "How do you know about them?"

This was going from bad to worse. "I met a djinn once, and I learned too late just how twisted his wishes actually were."

Olivia wasn't looking her in the eye any longer. "A-about Cedric…"

She really didn't want to talk about him. But Ella pulled her hand back and waited for the next question to come.

"If werewolves came from your-your wings…"

Not my wings. The wings of my friends. Family. Grief rose within her, nearly choking Olivia. "I had really piss poor taste in men."

Olivia's lashes flickered. "What about vampires?"

"What about them?" *You're one. You think I don't know? I do…but are you a djinn and a vamp?*

"Where did they come from? Did your kind—were they from your wings, too?"

Ella sighed as she remembered this. "No. I had a…a friend. Very long ago. She lost her wings but she didn't die. She married a human. Had children with him. And one of those children…*he* became the vampire. Our kind, you see, the fey, we drink blood. It gives us power. And her son inherited that trait from her. No wings," Ella murmured. "He wasn't full-blooded fey, so it makes sense that he didn't have the wings. He was what we became once the wings were gone. And once he was born as a vampire, he passed that trait down to others…spread it both through his bloodline, then, eventually, through the bite itself."

Olivia surged to her feet. "Your kind created vampires *and* werewolves?"

No, we didn't make them. Cedric did. In his never-ending-quest to change what I was. "You know," Ella told her as she tilted her head and studied the lady, "you seem really, really stressed. Do you want to talk about things?"

Olivia's lips parted. "I—"

The door flew open. "Tell me you didn't wish," Eric snarled as he filled that doorway. *"Tell me, Olivia."*

His eyes were so turbulent. And his jaw was clenched with his fury.

A fury directed at Olivia?

Ella found herself stepping in front of the other woman. "What is the deal with what she wished? Wishes are for children." *And for a Fey who doesn't want to spend eternity alone.* "They don't hurt—"

"She was a djinn before Shane transformed her," he gritted out, confirming Ella's fears with those hard words. "I'm not so sure that transformation took fully. Her wishes *are* granted. Only they're twisted all around."

Ella glanced over her shoulder, studying the woman with renewed interest. "How amazing." She smiled even as her heart constricted. "I met another djinn once. A few lifetimes ago." *They were supposed to all be dead, too. Guess none of us can stay in the ground.*

For just an instant, Ella remembered that long ago day. A traveling group had come through the area. The djinn had been there, selling wishes and dreams.

Because I went to him, so sad. Telling him that I hated to be alone. That I wished I had someone who would love me fully. Completely.

Madly.

And Cedric…he'd most definitely loved her *madly.*

"Olivia…" Eric pushed.

"Ella is the key!" Olivia cried out. "To everything! She's the reason the Pandora's Box of the paranormal opened."

Ella's shoulders stiffened. "Watch it, djinn. *Your* people were around long before I was. How do you think the fey ever came to be?"

Olivia stared at her with blank eyes.

"Someone wanted to live forever," Ella said. "Once upon a time…if the tales I heard were true…a wish was granted. But there were strings attached, because there always are. The blood was the price we paid. We always craved it, and in the end, the bloodlust ruled us."

She turned back to Eric. She tried to smile for him. "She thinks you aren't like me." Ella headed toward him, completely closing the distance that had separated them. Her hand lifted and stroked his cheek. "As if I wouldn't know you…"

His hand flew up and caught hers. "Ella…"

Footsteps rushed behind him. Ella saw Holly appear, and at the sight of the doctor, ice slid through her veins. "Eric, what's going on?"

But Holly ran around him. She glared at Ella. "Your blood. That's what's wrong. It's toxic."

Ella started to back away from Eric, but he just held her tighter. "No."

"I saw it in my tests." Holly swiped a hand over her cheek. *Wiping away tears?* "And now you've given that blood to Eric. You're going to kill him! You're going to—"

"Enough!" Eric nearly yelled. "Stop it, I told you, her blood won't kill me."

Ella felt a wobbly smile curl her lips. "I know that. It can't. You're just like me."

Sadness slid over his face. "No, baby. I'm sorry. The last thing I am is like you."

"You just don't know—"

"I made myself into something more, Ella."

She didn't like the way he was looking at her. There were too many emotions swirling in his gaze. Anger. Fear. Pity?

No, not pity, please.

"I had to be strong enough to fight the monsters, so I became one."

She yanked her hand away from him.

"I was dying in a battlefield when I went through the transformation. The first one. Shane came to me, and he gave me his blood. He saved me that day."

Shane.

And she remembered the dream that had come to her. Sand and blood and death. Not her dream. His.

"Shane opened my eyes to a whole new world of possibilities. I could be stronger. Faster. I just had to change. And I did change. I devoted my life to the Para Unit. When the docs there needed a guinea pig for their experiments, I signed up."

Ella hadn't signed up for the experiments that had been performed on her. She'd been locked in a dungeon. Trapped in golden chains.

"Then what are you?" Ella asked him as her heart broke.

"I am the monster that men made. Part vampire. Part werewolf. Science and magic blending all together. I can't shift, but I've got a werewolf's strength. I have fangs and I can drink blood…but only when necessary. Only in battle or—"

"Lust," Ella finished. Because passion had always stirred her need for blood. A dull ringing filled her ears. "You didn't…volunteer. You were made—"

"I volunteered," he said grimly. "I wanted every single change. I wanted to face the beast at the door head on. *I* did this."

She could only shake her head. "But I-I know you. When we were together, I felt…" Her words trailed away. Saying them was just too hard. *Whole. Complete.*

"I don't know what you felt." His Adam's apple bobbed as he swallowed. "But you're just responding to my screwed up DNA now. Maybe it's some trick because of all the things they did to me in the labs. Maybe…" He looked away from her. "It wasn't just about me being part werewolf and part vampire. There were other…things, too."

"Things? What *things?*" But she suspected and nausea filled her. Her hand rose to her shoulder, almost as if she could feel the wings behind her back. Dread rose within her, nearly choking Ella. "No…"

"Some of the stuff they had…it had been in government containment for years. It's possible…" Now his voice went gruff. "If the government was in possession of Fey wings, that could certainly explain some of the earlier experiments I saw. I saw and…*participated* in."

He was gutting her. Right there. Ella's knees gave way and she would have fallen to the floor if he hadn't lunged forward and grabbed her arms.

"That's how you knew," Ella managed to whisper. "About my wings…why the gold hurt me. Your government—they'd taken more of my kind? Experimented on them?" She was going to be sick. Violently sick.

But beneath that twisting, churning nausea…and the terrible ache of betrayal she felt as she stared at him, rage began to stretch and spread through her, snaking like vines through her body. Growing, growing…

"Cedric wanted to change me," Ella said. "He did. By the time he was done, my wings came out only when my anger took over fully. He'd bottled up the beast, but no beast likes its cage."

Eric tightened his hold on her. "I'm not trying to cage you. And I didn't know about the gold until Reece and the others attacked you. I swear, I'm not trying to lock you up!"

"Yes," it hurt to say the truth, "you are. Just as Cedric did. Just as Keegan did." And she'd been a blind fool. A man gave her pleasure instead of pain, and she hadn't been able to see past the moment. When would she learn the truth? There was no happiness to be found for her in this world.

It just wasn't there.

The rage grew even more when Eric wrapped his fingers around her shoulders. "You have to listen to me, Ella."

"I don't *have* to do anything." Fey had once been thought of as being nearly gods. Then they'd been decimated. After Cedric, others had realized that their wings contained power. They'd been hunted. Tracked down. And those wings had been sliced off. One at a time and the cries of the fey had filled the night.

Vengeance. Bloodlust. Death.

Evil. Yes, they'd attacked back in a force that had been savage.

It is our nature. "You can't bottle the beast," Ella said again and pain ripped through her. So sharp and hard that she jerked form Eric's hold and fell to her knees.

"Ella?" He was right beside her. His hands were reaching out to her again.

"No!" Ella yelled. "Don't touch me!" It hurt. It hurt so much. An agony that wouldn't stop. Cedric had made it hurt. He'd warped her.

Turned something that had been natural into this agony. Her wings were coming out now, fueled by her fury. She could feel the stretch along her shoulder blades. Could feel the skin starting to rip open as the wings pushed for freedom.

They were on the first floor of the building. The shrink's office had a window.

They will not contain me.

"Ella, Ella, sweetheart, I need you to calm down."

Her gaze shot to his.

She saw his eyes widen.

"Black," he whispered, "not blue. I didn't notice before…"

Her eye color change was the least of her concerns right then.

Holly had run out of the door and she was yelling for Connor and Shane. Ella's hands pushed against the floor, her palms digging in to the carpet as her back arched with the transformation.

"I never meant to hurt you," Eric said. "Sweetheart, I'm sorry."

Her teeth snapped together. "You should…go…"

"No, no, I'm staying right with you."

*He wants your wings…*A dark whisper from inside. *He knows what they can do. He's been playing you. He wants your fury to erupt and then he'll be taking those wings, slicing them right off your back.*

That wasn't possible. She shook her head. The thought had seemed so foreign. Just—not her at all.

But then she saw Connor rush into the room. And in his hands...

A golden net. The same net that Reece and his werewolf goons had used on her.

Her heart splintered. "Eric, no."

"What?" His head whipped around and he looked back at Connor. "Get that damn thing out of here, now!"

But it was too late. She wouldn't believe his lies any longer.

The wings ripped from her back as she shifted into the form she'd been so long ago. Her true form. A whip of wind filled the room, driven by her flapping wings as she rose from the floor and towered over the man who'd just cut out her heart.

He might not be her soul mate, but she'd been falling for him. And all along, he'd just wanted to cage her.

Trap her.

Keep her.

Use her.

"No one will...use me...again..."

Eric yanked the golden net from Connor's hands. Seeing it there—seeing Eric hold it broke something deep within Ella. She whirled and flew right toward the window.

"No!" Eric bellowed. "Ella, *don't leave me!"*

She flew straight through the heavy blind and the glass. The glass shattered around her, cutting into her skin and her wings, but she didn't care.

She just kept going.

She didn't look back.

***

"Ella!" Eric ran to the window. Glass crunched beneath his feet. "Don't!"

But she was gone. Flying fast and hard and right toward the sun.

Only she wasn't burning and she sure didn't seem weak. *Because she wasn't a vampire.* Never had been.

He still had the net in his hands. That stupid net. He looked down at it. "Why did you bring this?"

"Because Holly told me about your new girlfriend's toxic blood, I thought—"

Eric lost it. Just. Lost. It.

He whirled, the net dropping from his fingers and he lunged at Connor. In less than two seconds time, he had his friend pinned against the wall. Eric had one hand around Connor's throat and the other hand was a fist that was hurtling right toward Connor's face.

"Stop." Shane's voice. Shane wrapped his hand around Eric's wrist, stilling the movement. "You need to calm down. We all do. You're attacking a friend."

Slowly, Eric's head turned until he could face Shane. "He was going to attack *her*."

"*Containment*," Connor snapped. Eric's other hand was still tight around his throat so the word emerged as a gasp. "Just…containing…"

"No one will contain her again. She's been through that shit enough." But he made himself step back. He let Connor go.

Connor sucked in a deep gulp of air. "Since when…are you strong…enough to strangle…alpha…"

"Since long before you came into the picture." His laugh was bitter. But now they would all know the truth. He was the biggest monster they'd faced. The one with the most power. The one who'd spent too long pretending to be a man.

Even after his humanity was gone.

But Ella made me feel differently. She made me happy. She made me remember what it was like to be someone else.

"I know what you did," Olivia said, her voice a strained whisper.

Eric immediately whirled toward her. *She made the wish. She wanted Olivia to see the truth.* "You and your damned cursed wishes!"

Shane immediately stepped in his path. "There are some things that no one does…and *no one* talks to my Olivia that way."

Was he supposed to be afraid of the big, bad vampire? Shane had changed him once, but that had been long ago. And Eric had been through dozens of experiments since then. "And no one puts *my* Ella at risk! She's alone out there now. And that asshole—you all remember the one who killed Keegan right on our fucking doorstep?—he's out there. He'll be hunting her. We left her open to his attack!"

"It might not be an attack," Holly said.

His fangs were out, and he didn't give a shit. *I need to find Ella.* He stalked back to the window. He could smell her blood there and see it gleaming on the glass. She'd hurt herself when she'd fled from him.

"He may have no intention of hurting her," Holly said. Eric could hear her footsteps shuffling closer. "I mean…if he's really like her, then maybe he was the one she was searching for, anyway."

What? Eric glared at his sister.

"Another of her kind," Holly told him softly. "A male. If the mating drive for Ella…if it's anything like a werewolf's, then maybe the fey male thinks that she's his mate. The same way—"

"Ella thought I was hers."

Her expression was sad. "It happens. These instincts are primitive. Maybe he picked up her scent and realized there was a female of his kind out there."

His fangs were lengthening. And his muscles were straining. Stretching with his fury.

"Uh, Holly…" Connor began.

"That could even explain why the guy killed Keegan," she added. "Perhaps the male knew that Keegan had hurt Ella and wanted to protect her, it's the drive of nature and—"

Connor grabbed her arm. "Seriously, stop it. You're telling the guy that there's another male out there—one who actually *could* be Ella's real mate. He's about to flip the fuck out. Don't you see that?"

Her eyes widened, as if she were truly seeing him for the first time. "Eric?"

Holly. Sweet Holly. She'd never realized just how far gone he was. "I…needed her."

Holly backed up. "Why do you seem bigger?"

Because he was. His muscles had grown, his body had hardened—the beast wanted Ella back. "She brought me…peace."

Holly shook her head. "No, she's a threat, she—"

"I have to find her."

Not cage her, never that. Find her and convince her to stay. To give him a chance. No lies. No secrets.

No cages.

Fear rolled through him on a wave that seemed to make his vision dim for a moment. It wasn't safe for Ella to be out there alone. There could still be other members of Keegan's pack who wanted to hunt her. If they knew about what her wings could do—and Eric suspected they did—others would go after her. It wouldn't be safe.

"Easy…" Shane said as he approached Eric with his hands up. "Once a vampire tastes his prey, he can track her anywhere. You know you can find her."

"I'm not a vampire." So much more. "I can't track her that way." But there was another method he could use even as the thought of what he'd done sent a spike of shame through him. He'd tagged her—had Holly put that tracking device beneath her skin. Ella didn't know about that betrayal, not yet.

As long as the device stayed hidden, he could find her.

He *would* find her.

CHAPTER TEN

She perched on the top of an old church. One that looked as if it had been abandoned long ago. The sun was behind her, and Ella knew she should seek shelter inside. Not because the rays of the sun would hurt her. She didn't have a vampire's weakness that way. But because humans might see her. Humans might freak out.

Humans…

The fey had thought that humans were never really any sort of threat. And Ella, so long ago, she'd been curious about them. Then she'd met Cedric. Handsome, charming, smart Cedric. She'd given him her heart, even though she'd been raised to believe that she must mate with her own kind. That she had to keep her precious bloodline going.

Only now there is no bloodline. There's nothing.

Ella had tried to explain to Cedric that centuries could pass and she wouldn't age, but he would. She hadn't wanted to watch him wither and die—she hadn't wanted to see his pain at all.

When the elders gave the order that she had to leave him…

Cedric changed everything.

He'd gone after her with that golden net. She'd been the one to reveal that weakness to him. He'd tossed that net over her. Kept her prisoner in his castle. He'd sent out his men…so many humans…and they'd been armed with gold, too.

Suddenly, the humans had been very much a threat.

Her eyes closed. For just an instant, she was back there with him…

"Cedric, please, release me!" The gold had burned her wings and she'd been in so much agony.

"You were going to leave me. Me? After promising me your heart?" His brown eyes had glittered with his fury. His handsome face had been a hard mask. A stranger had stood before her. *"Not after all I did to acquire you."*

Acquire. That one word had pounded through her.

"We can't be together," Ella had told him softly. *"I don't die, Cedric. I can't – "*

"Your kind will die. I'll see to it."

Fear had burst through her. So much fear. *"No, please!"*

"You will all beg me before I am done." His hand had slipped through the net and curled under her

chin. *"I was meant to have your power. I was meant to live forever. And I will find a way."* He'd smiled at her. *"Fey are too flawed. Too arrogant. Too rage-filled. I will change them. I will change you. And then you will be mine, forever."*

No…

Her eyes opened. The past vanished. Cedric had kept his word. He had changed her. He had changed all the fey. And her kind had died.

But she hadn't been his. She'd gotten out of that castle and left fire in her wake. She'd burned the place to the very ground.

Another fire.

Just like the one that had taken Keegan.

Two men who'd held her captive. Two men who'd lost their lives.

And now…now there was Eric.

Her wings stretched behind her. She flew off that chapel and broke through one of the stained-glass windows of that old church. She barely registered the shattering of the glass.

Her feet touched down on the dirty, dusty floor. Her arms wrapped around her stomach. Why had she been so very certain that Eric was the one? Because he'd altered his body, his very genetic structure, and her senses had been fooled?

She sat on the ground. Her wings fluttered around her as her head sagged forward.

Maybe it hadn't been her senses that were fooled. Maybe her heart had been the problem.

A heart that had been fooled by a human once.

And now again.

Fool me once, shame on you…

Fool me twice…

A tear slipped down her cheek.

Shame on me.

***

"Damn. That lady can sure fly fast and hard." Connor gave a low whistle as he stared down at the laptop screen in front of him. Eric kept his foot shoved down on the gas pedal as he hurtled the SUV down the road. "According to this, she's over thirty miles away."

Hell. He hadn't wanted to go in with a full team. The last thing Eric wanted to do was spook her. He just wanted to talk with Ella. To convince her that she didn't need to run from him.

"I still think we should have brought the net," Connor said.

Eric's hands tightened around the wheel. "She isn't the enemy."

"Is that your brain talking?" Connor asked bluntly. "Or your dick?"

He just growled back.

"Thought so," Connor muttered. "Choice number three. Your heart?"

"Screw that shit. You know the stories. I don't have a heart."

"I know bull when I hear it. You're hot to get this woman back, not because you think she could be some asset to the Para Unit, but because you just want her close—close to you. She's incredibly dangerous, and, by her own account, her kind are *evil*. You told me the same shit just a few hours ago. Fey play with humans. They can't be trusted."

"Ella and I have a deal. She'll stick to the deal. So will I."

"Turn right up ahead," Connor said calmly.

He jerked the wheel to the right and kept flooring the gas.

Connor's right hand flew out and locked around the dashboard as the tires squealed. "Sonofabitch," Connor groused. "We're strong, but we can still get hurt man. I don't want to go flying through the windshield today."

And he didn't want Ella flying away. "Is her signal still at the same location?"

"Just where it's been for the last five minutes. I think your girl has found her some shelter for the day. Now we just need to get there…and see if she tries to kill you or not."

"She won't."

"Uh, her wings came out. Isn't that supposed to be some big sign that she's all raging-up?"

Maybe. Yes. No. Shit, he didn't know. "She was hurt. I hurt her."

"Because you lied?"

He should have brought Shane with him. Or maybe even Lawrence. Sure, Lawrence was human, but the guy was cool under pressure. And he didn't ask a million freaking questions. "Stop pushing me, dammit. I didn't lie, I just—"

"Pulled a Pate? Mislead? Got her to do what *you* wanted?" Connor's laughter was a bit cold. "You tagged her, man. Like she was some kind of animal. And we're tracking her. I realize you haven't dated in a while, but this really isn't the way this shit works."

He shot Connor a glare.

"How do you think she's going to react when she realizes you put a tracking chip under her skin?"

"Can I just deal with one fucking problem at a time?" Eric snarled back. Jesus. He had to get to Ella first. He had to talk to her. Had to convince her not to fly away and leave him. Again.

And until he did convince her of that, he wouldn't be talking about the chip. *Because it's my only way to find her.*

"Lies never work, man. Take that bit of advice from a guy who has been there." A pause. Then, Connor said, "Go left at the light. But, seriously, slow the fuck down before you make that turn."

He did slow the fuck down. A bit. Then he made the turn. And he also had to ask, "How the hell are you holding up?"

The temperature in the car seemed to ice. "What's that supposed to mean?" Connor asked.

"Keegan's dead."

"Yeah, and so what? That's one less threat to my Chloe, one less—"

"He was your brother." A brother that Connor hadn't known about, not until the guy had come around and started killing.

"He was a twisted psychopath," Connor replied flatly. "And the world is safer without him."

But that still doesn't tell me how you're doing. If he hadn't been so torn up over Ella, then Eric would have pushed the guy. Instead, he just pushed the accelerator down more.

They traveled in silence for a time until Connor spoke again. "Something else for you to consider…if Ella does go all Fey crazy, what will you do?"

"It's not going to happen."

"You don't know that. Just like I didn't know Keegan would be freaking insane." His breath heaved out. "So you need to plan ahead. If she goes crazy, if she attacks you or humans…what will you do? Will you really be able to send her off to Purgatory?"

He'd taken over Purgatory. Put *his* men in charge there. He'd gotten the power straight from the federal government after the place had gone to hell in a hand basket. There would be no more uprisings in the prison. The inmates would be treated civilly. Olivia was even working on possible rehabilitation programs…

If one could rehabilitate monsters who thirsted for blood and death.

"I don't think you can do it," Connor said, his voice rough. "And that is a big damn problem."

Eric locked his jaw. "It's not going to come to that."

"We'd better hope not."

***

She heard him coming before she saw him.

At the faint sound of footsteps, Ella tensed. Then, in the next instant, she shot to her feet. Someone was coming toward her, a man—she could catch his scent in the air. Masculine, slightly wild, woodsy.

Not Eric.

And surely that wasn't disappointment she felt, now was it? She hadn't actually expected him to rush after her, apologizing on his knees, telling her how wrong he was?

Maybe.

Her wings had vanished again. Her back ached a bit, and she knew her shirt was pretty much ripped to pieces in the rear. She could feel the air against her spine. But the front of the shirt was mostly in place. She wasn't flashing anything she shouldn't be.

And the guy–

He was closing in.

Had he seen her fly into the old church? Was he coming to investigate?

Her gaze flew around. She could hide. Or she could–

"You don't need to run from me."

A shudder slid along her body. No way.

Absolutely *no way…*

Her gaze flew to the church's doors. Doors that she knew had been locked. She'd seen the heavy chain herself. But now those doors were open. And that masculine, woodsy scent was a whole lot stronger.

Because he was there.

Still handsome. Still young. Still strong.

When he should have been dead and buried centuries ago.

Tall, dark and handsome. No new lines were on his face. His jaw was just as hard. His shoulders and body just as powerful as always.

"C-Cedric?" Ella's voice trembled. Both from fear and from straight-up shock.

He smiled at her. *Same smile.* "Hello, love. It's been too long."

No, no this could *not* be happening. "You aren't here." Had she finally gone crazy? Another side effect of living forever…sometimes your mind just wasn't as strong as your body. No matter what you did…

Something broke, sooner or later.

She laughed. Her eyes were wide open and she was still seeing the past.

He walked toward her. The sound of his footsteps echoed around them.

Her laughter faded. His hand lifted and touched her cheek. She gasped at that contact, because his touch took her right back to the dungeon he'd kept her in.

Another man. Another hell.

Her body froze as she stared up at him. "You're here."

He smiled at her. A wide, slow grin. The grin that had first charmed her so long ago. "Of course, I am. I found you."

Her body was frozen, her limbs stiff with shock, but her heart was racing frantically in her chest. "You can't be here."

He laughed. "Oh, my beautiful, Ella…I told you that we were meant to be. I was always meant to be more than a man." And now she could see the fangs peeking just behind his lips. "And you were always meant to be mine."

She jumped back from him, putting a fast distance between their bodies. "You're a vampire?"

"No."

He didn't follow her. Just watched her.

"You *are* a vampire." It made sense. "That's how you're still alive. That's—"

"Your elders said you had to mate with one of your own kind. I couldn't let you go to another…so I killed all of them."

Nausea hit her. Cold, shattering. The guilt—the guilt she'd carried for centuries—rose once more to nearly choke her. *My fault. All of them. Because I fell for a monster even worse than me.*

"Fey were vicious and cold, so I just had to be more vicious. I had to be colder. Crueler." He shrugged. "I was."

A vehicle's engine growled outside. Her gaze jumped toward the open doorway. She didn't even know how long she'd been in that church. She'd huddled on the ground for far too long, her wings around her, tears on her cheeks. Then she'd looked up and the wings had been gone.

The rage—gone.

She'd been empty.

"You wanted a mate. Someone just like you." He spread his arms wide. "And I was always right there. You didn't realize it then. You *ran* from me."

Centuries had passed. If he'd been out there, all that time…

His jaw hardened. "I searched the world for you. I followed and followed, but you were always one step ahead of me. So frantic. I knew what you were doing. You were trying to find someone else to mate. Someone that would match you. But you already had me."

"No, You're not…" *Not my mate. Not anything.*

Car doors slammed. Footsteps rushed toward them.

"I killed the one who hurt you. Do you want me to tell you how he begged before I dropped him? How he pleaded with me?"

Ella shook her head. New scents had reached her, and she was terrified. *That's Eric out there. He can't face Cedric.*

"He thought he would make you his captive again. The fool believed your power would be his." Cedric began to advance. He seemed so totally focused on her. Had he even heard the car's approach? "I wasn't going to let him hurt you again. I protected you. Just as I will do for the rest of our very long lives." He smiled once more. And he offered her his hand. "I missed you."

She stared at his hand as she backed up. The hand that had imprisoned her. The hand that had tortured her. The hand that had injected her with who the hell knew what in his monstrous castle. She'd begged and begged to be let go. She'd begged and begged for him to free the other fey.

She'd begged.

No more.

Her hand slid down and curled around an old church pew. The wood was broken. She just needed to yank it loose a bit more…

"I dreamed of you, Ella."

"And I had nightmares about you."

His smile slipped.

"Ella!"

At Eric's shout, Cedric whipped around—and she saw his back for the first time.

His wings were back there, curled down so she hadn't seen them before. Full wings. Powerful. Strong.

Now those wings were stretching out. Dark and big—a Fey's wings.

Wings that he shouldn't have.

She yanked harder on that wood, and a chunk broke loose in her hand. "Get back!" Ella yelled to Eric. She shot to the side, trying to see him around Cedric's body. *"Get out of here!"*

But Eric wasn't fleeing. He stood in the doorway, his legs braced apart, and Connor was right behind him.

"Told you we should've brought that gold net," Connor said. "Now there are *two* of them."

The gold net?

Cedric glanced at her. "See, my love. To them, you are a beast. Nothing more. Bet they want to lock you up."

"You mean like you did?" Ella retorted. No one had attacked. Not yet. Good. She'd be the one drawing first blood. Ella kept the chunk of wood hidden behind her leg as she slowly advanced on Cedric. "I was just a beast to you, too. You think I don't know that? You just wanted to take my power away. It was never about me."

But he shook his head and his dark gaze hardened. "You are my key. My everything. I *will* have you." He flew toward her with a sudden burst of speed.

And Ella slammed the chunk of wood into his chest. "Guess what? We broke up. *Centuries* ago. In case you didn't get the message."

Blood darkened his shirt and he let out a terrible bellow, one that seemed to shake the very church.

"Ella…" Cedric said her name with a twisted combination of fury and desire. "You haven't changed. Still so blood-thirsty…"

She stared at his wings. "You've changed plenty."

"I changed *for* you." He yanked the wood out of his chest and tossed it onto the floor. "I became what you wanted."

"No…" She shook her head—and then she dove for cover.

Because she'd seen Eric pulling out his weapon. Eric *and* Connor and she'd distracted Cedric so that they would have time to fire.

And fire they did. The sound of blasting bullets filled the air. Cedric roared and whirled toward them.

The bullets hit him right in the chest. Again and again and—

Silence.

Cedric fell to the ground.

Dead? No, that wouldn't be so easy. She could see the slow rise and fall of his chest.

"Since the tranqs didn't take him down last time," Eric called out. "I got Holly to add a little something extra to the mix for him."

She had a feeling that "something extra" might be gold. Enough gold so that he would be weakened and the drugs could take effect.

And now Eric and Connor still had their weapons out. They seemed to be aimed right at her.

She was crouched on the floor, her hands curled into fists. "Will you shoot me next?"

Eric gave a hard, negative shake of his head. He holstered his weapon and hurried toward her.

"But you came armed," Ella said. "So what was your plan?"

He stood in front of her now. Just as Cedric had done, Eric offered his hand to her.

Ella didn't take it. She rose slowly and her knees trembled a bit. But she didn't need him to steady her. Ella steadied herself.

"Call for back-up," Eric ordered Connor. "We're going to need a transport team."

She glanced over at Cedric. His eyes were closed. His wings still spread behind him.

"I guess you found another of your kind," Eric told her, voice gruff.

Feeling oddly numb, Ella shook her head. "No. I found the mad scientist. He just became the monster."

"What?"

She crept away from Eric. Connor was crouched beside Cedric, checking his pulse. "You need to be careful with him," she said. Even her voice sounded odd. Too cold and flat. "He's very, very dangerous."

"So are we," Eric said. He'd lowered his hand, but he hadn't backed away.

"He must have been watching the base," Ella said, trying to puzzle things through. "And he followed me here."

"You know him." Now emotion had entered Eric's voice. Seething. Hard. "This 'mad scientist'—"

"Why can't anyone just be happy as they are? You changed. He changed. Why? For more power? To be the biggest badass in the room?" She just didn't get it. "I used to long to be normal.

To have the lives that humans did. They were happy. They didn't have to constantly fight the bloodlust. The need to attack. To kill. He said he'd make me better, but Cedric just made himself worse."

Eric whirled toward the slumped figure on the ground. "This is Cedric? Your damn ex-lover?"

Jealousy. Why would Eric pretend to feel that emotion? She rubbed her temples. "How did you find us?" True mates—fey mates—were supposed to be able to track each other any place. Hope stirred within her. Ridiculous. She tried to squash it.

Eric and Connor shared a dark look, but neither spoke.

More secrets.

"Our deal is over," Ella said quietly. How long would it take their transport team to arrive? With the Para Unit, it could be mere minutes before others swarmed. Before that swarming happened, she intended to be long gone. "You got Keegan. You have his pack. I'm done."

She started to walk past him. But Eric's hand flew out and wrapped around her. He pulled her up against him, their bodies too close. "We're not done," he growled.

"Eric…" Connor said, his voice tight.

But Eric didn't look away from her. "Our deal isn't over."

"What more do you want?"

"Uh, Eric, seriously…" Connor's voice sharpened.

"Everything," Eric told her. "I need—"

"The bastard is awake!" Connor yelled.

Eric grabbed Ella and shoved her behind his back. She craned her neck to the side and saw Cedric shoot up—right into the air. Then he spun toward her and Eric.

Eric had his gun out and aimed once more. "What the hell does it take…" Eric demanded, "to put you down?"

Cedric grinned back at him. "More than you've got." Then his gaze slid to Ella. "Want me to kill them for you, love? I can do it. Right here. Right now."

Horrified, she screamed, "No!"

And that must have been the wrong answer.

His grin vanished in a blink. "Why does he carry your scent, Ella?"

Oh, crap.

Connor started firing at him again. Cedric didn't even glance his way. His eyes—eyes that were *glowing* now—were on Ella. "Why do you want him to live, Ella? Why is he *touching* you, Ella?"

"Because I fucking want to," Eric shouted back. And he opened fire. The bullets slammed into Cedric. One. Two. Three.

His wings struggled to flap, and Cedric fell. He hit hard and slammed into the floor with an impact that made the whole church shudder.

"Fuck me," Connor muttered. "He doesn't stay down long."

Ella was shaking. *My wings aren't out. Why aren't my wings out?*

If her wings didn't come out, she couldn't flee. But there wasn't enough rage building inside of her. There was fear and sadness.

Too much sadness.

And then she realized just what had happened to her.

Eric turned toward her. "We're getting you out of here. The team is coming in with gold—they'll secure him, but I swear, they won't hurt you."

She could only shake her head. "You've already hurt me." So much so that there was no room for her rage any longer. "Eric, I think you broke my heart."

He flinched. And his hand came up to cup her chin. He kissed her. Fast and hard and almost desperately. "Then I *will* fix it, I swear."

Another lie. As if she could believe him now.

Cedric let out a groan.

Still looking at her, Eric shot him again. "Load him down with tranq," Eric said to Connor. "I don't want this bastard opening his eyes again until he's in containment."

Containment.

The ache in her chest just got worse. She didn't think it was possible to fix a heart. Not when it had been ripped apart.

CHAPTER ELEVEN

The prisoner was secured with gold chains. Chains that bound his ankles and his wrists. Those chains were heavy and thick, and they were locked to the stones that made up the floor of Cedric Wallington's cell.

"My, my," Cedric drawled as he tilted back his head and stared at Eric. "You sure do move fast. Was it Ella who told you about the Fey's weakness? Or was it those sick werewolves that I saw you bring into this place?"

Eric stared at him. He was in Cedric's cell. He'd been in there for the last twenty minutes, waiting for the bastard to open his eyes. Cedric's body still slumped on the floor, but Eric saw the way his arms and legs tensed.

The guy was about to prepare an attack.

It wouldn't work.

You didn't notice the collar yet, did you, buddy? Eric kept his hand behind his back. And he made sure to keep the remote control hidden.

"I'm betting it was the werewolves," Cedric mused. "You still have Keegan's crew here, don't you? That scarred asshole Reece…figured he'd be the weak link."

"So you know him…you know them all…" The fact that this jerk could speak so easily of the pack that had hunted Ella—

"They're on my kill list," Cedric said as he rose. He pushed back his shoulders and seemed to stretch a bit against his chains. "I always try to learn as much as possible about my enemies. I've found it very…helpful."

Eric just watched him. "I like to learn about my enemies, too."

Cedric's lips curved the faintest bit. "Do you want to know how you'll die?"

"Not particularly."

"I'll cut your heart out. While you watch. And then, for shits and giggles, I'll give it to Ella. And we'll just see how much she likes you then."

Eric kept his face expressionless. "You won't be getting anywhere near Ella. Not ever again."

Cedric surged forward, but he didn't get past three feet before those chains jerked him back. "She is *mine!* I spent centuries looking for her. Hunting. Tracking. Killing anyone in my path. I earned her. I bled and burned and died for her…"

Died?

"You look pretty alive to me," Eric murmured. *She's not yours. She won't ever be.*

Cedric's gaze swept over him. "So do you, but we both know the truth. I'm what Ella seeks. Another of her kind. And you…you're just someone else who is in my way."

Now was the time to push the bastard. "She called you a mad scientist. Ella told me all about you."

Uncertainty came and went on the guy's face.

"She said you were crazy. That you hurt the fey and yet, here you are…claiming to be one of them."

"I changed, for her."

"I think you changed for yourself. Because you were a power hungry asshole who got off on other people's pain."

Cedric's booming laughter filled the room. "Well…" he finally said. "I guess it takes one…to know one…"

Don't kill him. Not yet. Eric's fingers slid over the remote. "What did you do to Ella? When you had her in that castle?"

Cedric's eyes turned to angry slits. "Everything she begged me to do."

Don't. Kill. Him.

But he sure wanted to.

"She loved me, did she *tell* you that?" Cedric asked, mocking now. "When you fucked her, did she call my name? Because I'm the one she wanted. The one she *should* have been with…if those Fey elders hadn't been so convinced that she had to wait for another mate. I *became* perfect for her. I became everything she wanted."

Eric lifted his brows. "Oh, sorry, I guess I missed that whole perfection bit when she was shoving that stake into your chest. My bad."

Cedric lunged forward again.

This time, Eric did hit the remote.

Cedric screamed and fell to his knees.

"Know what that is?" Eric asked him, voice cool and almost conversational. He was rather proud of the tone, especially considering the fury pumping through his veins. "That's gold. *In* you. I can make you hurt more…" He pressed the button. Another scream echoed around him. "Or I can make you hurt less." And he stopped the flow. "We usually just use silver collars, but I thought it prudent to have a gold one made up…"

Cedric's head lifted once more, but he didn't rise from the floor. "You didn't know about me. Not until…" His breath heaved out. "Today." A muscle clenched in his jaw. Sweat covered his forehead. "Was the collar…for Ella?"

"The collar was a precaution."

"You want to…cage her…too."

"No."

"She won't…be yours. You aren't her match." The guy's voice was getting stronger.

And Eric was getting annoyed. "I'm getting really sick of this mating talk. I get it with the werewolves. Biology. Genetics. Blah-the-fuck. But I make my own rules. I don't worry about fate. *I* change things."

Cedric nodded. "So…do I." Very slowly, he pushed back to his feet, but he made no move to attack Eric. "Guess we're more…alike than you realized."

"I am nothing like you. I haven't killed a whole race of beings—"

"I know about your Purgatory. You just think you can lock us all up and throw away the key." His voice was definitely stronger now. Eric made a mental note of just how long the guy's weakness had lasted. "Won't work. Eventually, they'll get out." His gaze turned distant. "They always do."

"Because Ella got away from you? She escaped? And the others…did any of them get away, too?"

Cedric closed his eyes and inhaled. "Her scent doesn't belong on you. Don't touch her again."

It was Eric's turn to laugh. "I'll do whatever the hell…" Now his voice lowered, "*She* wants."

Then he turned away. He was done with that bastard for the moment.

"She doesn't want you! Ella is always looking—because she thinks it was her fault! If she'd been with the mate her elders had predicted, they would have all been safe."

Eric stopped.

"She'll always look for him. She thinks to atone."

Eric glanced over his shoulder.

"I know her," Cedric said. "I understand her. She thinks her greatest mistake was loving me."

Eric's teeth ground together. "You'll never see her again."

"She's wrong, though," he said, as if Eric hadn't spoken. "Her greatest mistake…was ever caring about the other Fey at all. *That* was her weakness. And it will be again. I tried to fix her. But she was already damaged, all along."

The hell she was. "Ella is perfect. And you won't ever hurt her again." Then, because he was fucking pissed, his fingers jammed on the remote once more.

The guy's scream followed him out of that cell.

The door shut behind him with a heavy clang.

And Connor was standing in the hallway, waiting.

"I guess the gold collar works," Connor murmured, voice mild.

Eric tossed it to him. "Yeah, it works."

Connor's hand closed around the remote. "Holly sure moved fast on these. When did you give the order to make them?"

"It was easy to do. Just use liquid gold instead of the silver that we normally have with the werewolves."

Connor stepped into his path. "When did you give the order to make them?" he asked again.

Dammit. "After I saw how Ella reacted to the golden net, okay? When I realized how powerful she was."

Connor swore.

"I wasn't planning to use it on her!" Judging by his expression, Connor didn't believe him. Eric straightened his shoulders. "At the time, I thought, if Ella exists…" He exhaled and raked a hard hand through his hair. "Others could, too. We needed to be ready." He looked back at the shut door. "Want to tell me I was wrong?"

"No, you're not wrong," Now there was a quiet rage in Connor's voice. "But you sure are one cold-blooded bastard."

***

Ella stared at Olivia. Olivia stared back.

Sighing, Ella said, "I get it. He left me with you because he thought I might be less likely to freak out and attack a shrink. Don't worry. I won't wing out and go for your throat."

A faint line appeared between Olivia's brows. "I wasn't worried about that."

"No? I was," she confessed.

Olivia almost smiled. "Do you know why Eric brought me on as part of his unit?"

"Because someone had to talk to the crazy paranormals? And paranormal shrinks aren't exactly thick on the ground?"

Olivia shook her head. "Because I knew that not all paranormals were true monsters. I understood that every being is different. Sometimes, there are just…triggers…that can send some down a dark path."

"A dark path," Ella repeated. "Guess that's one way of looking at things."

Sadness came and went in Olivia's eyes. "You're not evil, Ella."

She stiffened. "I don't like being analyzed."

"You think you are. Maybe you try to act that way…because you're punishing yourself."

Ella shook her head. "A girl's crazy ex shows up and everyone thinks—"

"That you blame yourself for what he did? Do you, Ella? Do you blame yourself for what happened to the Fey?"'

She looked down at her hands. "I brought Cedric into our world. He was a warlord. I should have known he only had one thought—power. Conquer and take power."

"You can't control someone else's actions."

Ella jumped to her feet. "Okay, this little chat is fun and all but—"

"You're punishing yourself."

"I'm not."

"You seek out danger. When Keegan first captured you…how did that happen?"

"Oh, yeah, total win, doc. Way to blame the victim there."

Olivia blanched. "I didn't mean—"

Whatever. "I'd heard that Keegan was working with some corrupt senator—that he was capturing innocent paranormals and not sending them to Purgatory, but keeping them in some sick secondary prison. A place where *he* conducted experiments on them."

Olivia's eyes widened.

Ella shrugged. "So I acted like I was a weaker paranormal. I let myself get caught…but only so I could get in there and destroy the place. Which I did. Really, really well by the way." She could still remember the power of the rage that had swept through her. "You should have seen what they were doing to them in there." Her hand ran over her face. "Nope. Change that. It was better *not* to see it. Trust me."

The door opened. The prickle of awareness on her nape told her that Eric had just entered the room. She didn't look at him, though. Ella kept talking.

"I destroyed that secondary prison. A place that *never* should have existed, but Keegan and his goons couldn't help but notice my power. My wings. I created a distraction so the other paranormals could flee, but I didn't count on just how many pack mates Keegan had. They ran me down. They caught me." Her sweaty hands rubbed against her jeans—they'd given her fresh clothes when she came back in to the base. "And the rest, well, I think we all know how that particular story ends."

Olivia's gaze was oddly warm. Sympathetic. Patient. "You've never said…when Keegan held you captive, did he…assault you?"

"I'd consider starvation and torture—"

"Did he rape you, Ella?" The doc cut right to chase.

The temperature in the room seemed to drop. To just straight-up ice. Just where was that chill coming from?

She glanced over at Eric.

His eyes…They'd gone absolutely arctic.

"Ella?" Olivia pressed, then she followed Ella's stare and tensed. "We should be alone. Eric, leave so—"

Ella gazed into Eric's eyes. "He didn't rape me. No. He wasn't interested in me that way. Keegan just wanted my blood and my power. Nothing more." And, yes, she considered that a very lucky break. Because she'd been so helpless back then.

I don't ever want to be helpless again.

Eric's face seemed absolutely tormented. "I want *you* to leave us, Olivia." Even his voice was different. Gruff. Hoarse.

Olivia hesitated. "I'm not sure that's a good idea."

"It's a terrible idea," Ella agreed. "But you should go." She and Eric—they had to clear the air. She'd flown away from the guy.

He'd rushed after her.

And when Cedric had attacked, Eric had put his body in front of hers.

Liar. Betrayer.

Protector.

Lover?

Her chest still ached as she looked at him. But running away, that wasn't an answer—that had just been her rage and pain driving her to flee. She was way calmer now.

She hoped.

"Be careful with her," Olivia told Eric before she marched for the door.

A twisted smile pulled at Ella's lips. "Everyone sure seems to think I'll attack you."

The door closed behind Olivia. Eric shook his head. "That wasn't what she meant. She was warning *me* not to hurt you."

Ella's laugh was high and bitter. "Right. Because your friends care about what happens to me."

"They do care. Just like I care." He advanced.

She retreated, then absolutely hated herself for it. She stiffened her spine and lifted her chin. "You were interrogating Cedric."

His jaw clenched. "Yes."

"What are you going to do with him?"

"I don't know yet."

"Liar, liar," Ella taunted. "You're already thinking about sending him to Purgatory, aren't you?"

"Purgatory isn't for him. It wasn't designed to keep in prisoners who can fly. That kind of defeats the whole isolation and no-access-except-by-air-and-sea thing I had going on with the place."

She blinked.

"My first goal is to learn his secrets. When I have a new enemy, that's always step one."

Her hands felt clammy. She barely stopped herself from pushing them against her jeans again. "Is that what you did with me? Try to learn my secrets?"

He hesitated.

And she had her answer. "That's why you didn't push me, isn't it? You tried to build trust first." *Fool.* "You read me like a book. You saw that interrogations wouldn't work, so you tried to get beneath my guard. You let me believe—"

She whirled away, unable to look at him any longer. It just hurt too much.

"Ella, I never said I was Fey."

She gave a short, hard shake of her head. "That's not what I meant. Screw that. You let me believe that you actually wanted me. You even had sex with me to—"

His hands curled around her shoulder and he spun her right back around to face him. "That wasn't a lie."

She could only shake her head again.

"That wasn't a lie." His hold tightened on her. "I wanted you more than I'd ever wanted anything in my life. If I hadn't been with you then, right the fuck then, I think I would have gone insane."

"Lies," she whispered. "More—"

He kissed her.

She bit him.

A mistake. Oh, such a mistake. Because when her teeth nipped his lower lip, he gave a rough, ragged growl of desire. That sound shot right through her. And as his taste slid onto her tongue, lust burst within her.

"Just like right now," Eric muttered against her mouth. "I want you so damn much. Every moment, I want you."

She shoved against his shoulders. He let her go. But she could see the hunger glittering in his eyes.

Maybe that desire hadn't been a lie, after all.

"Control," Eric said, the word seemingly torn from him. "That's what my life has been about ever since I went through the transformations. I'm too strong. I can hurt others far too easily. I have to keep my control in place. Every moment. All the time."

She licked her lower lip and still tasted him. Her body ached. She yearned.

And it was wrong. They were wrong.

She'd gone down a dark path before with one lover. That path had ended in blood and death and fire.

Another wrong choice…

"I need to get away from you," Ella told him.

He staggered back a step. For just an instant, she saw pain flash across his face. Real pain. The kind that cuts open your soul and leaves you gutted.

Provided, of course, that you had a soul to begin with.

"You probably do," Eric said, shocking her. "But…" His voice roughened even more. "I am begging you not to leave."

What? "Stop it." Another trick. She doubted he'd ever begged for anything. Certainly not for her. This was just another—

"*Please.* I want you to stay. I need you to stay." He caught her hand in his and lifted it to his chest. Eric put her hand over his heart. "It beats differently when you're near me."

No. He had to—"Stop."

"Not faster. Not slower. Stronger. I feel different when you're near me. When I held you in my arms and you just slept—fucking *slept*—that was the most peace I'd had since I died on that blood-soaked mission in the Middle East. I thought I'd never know peace again. I thought all I had was the job. And then…there was you."

She had to blink quickly so her tears wouldn't fall. She didn't want him seeing her cry.

"I'm not a good man. Not the kind who follows the straight and narrow. I've seen too much darkness for that. I break rules. I get my hands dirty. I do whatever it takes to get the job done."

Am I a job?

No…no…he'd *begged.*

She didn't want him begging. She didn't want anyone begging.

Because I begged Cedric once. I begged him to stop hurting me. I begged him to let the Fey go.

"I was a monster long before I started to change. And the control that I hold so tightly? Sometimes, I think that's all that keeps me from winding up in Purgatory. Or, it was…until you."

"I don't understand…"

"I can let go with you, and not be afraid I'll wreck and destroy. I can let go with you…and not lose the last damn shred of humanity I have. I can just…let go. *With you.*"

Her hand was still over his heart. Heat from his body wrapped around her.

"I want you to be able to let go, with me," Eric told her. His eyes—they were swirling with emotion. One instant, they appeared a dark green. In the next, almost closer to blue. Was that color change a side effect of his transformations? Maybe some kind of tie to his emotions?

Her emotions were sure all over the place right then. She wanted to get far away from Eric. And she wanted to get as close as possible.

"Rage, fear, desire…" He exhaled raggedly. "I don't want you to hold anything back. I want you to show me all that you are, and, sweetheart, I'll do the same. No one knows me like you do. No one will ever know me that way." His mouth tightened "We aren't mates. Fuck me, but I wish we were. I wish I was that genetic match you need. Because that would be a tie that would help to keep you with me."

"Eric—" She stopped, not even sure what to say.

"But I'm not. I'm a man who messed with science and magic and became something else. And you…you are the most perfect woman I've ever seen."

No, not perfect. "I'm evil, I'm death, I leave destruction in my path, and I—"

He lifted her hand to his lips and kissed her fingers. Tenderly. "You brought me hope when I was sure I'd never have it again. Peace. *You* gave me that. I don't care what stories you were told. I don't care what happened before. You and me. Here and now. We matter. Fuck fate. We can choose our own path. Together."

Her heart was racing too fast. Her breath coming too quickly. He was offering her the most sinful temptation.

"Be with me again, Ella," Eric said, his voice a deep rumble that seemed to sink through her. "Be with me and let go of everything else."

She shouldn't.

She should leave. Walk—run—or fly away as fast as she could.

But what would she be running to? And wouldn't she always be looking back? Looking—for him?

"I will never betray you," Eric told her.

She moved fast as she made her decision, grabbing his shirtfront in her hands and fisting the material as she yanked him toward her. "You'd better not," she warned him. "Because hell truly doesn't compare to a Fey's fury."

Then Ella kissed him. Her mouth was open, hungry, and just as desperate as his when they came together.

Desire exploded between them.

She let her control go. Let emotions surge through her. Fury. Lust. Fear.

Hope.

She just let go…

And Eric was there to hold her tight.

***

Cedric pulled at the collar on his neck, but there was no give in the freaking thing. It didn't burn his fingers when he touched it, so he knew the gold was inside the collar, protected somehow.

"Might as well stop," a growling voice said.

His head snapped up. He saw the male standing in the doorway. Dark hair. Gold eyes. Predatory grin.

"I've got first-hand experience with those collars," the guy told him. "Save yourself some trouble. Don't try to get loose. It's not going to happen."

"I need to see Ella."

"Yeah, about that…" He sighed. "In case you didn't hear Pate, that won't be happening. Ella isn't coming anywhere near you."

"Yes, she is." He wasn't going to get this close—after so long—and have her slip away. "Bring her to me, *now*."

The man laughed. "Something tells me that Ella is a bit busy at the moment. Last I saw, Pate was rushing to be at her side." The fellow gave a little salute. "Enjoy the chains. I think they'll be keeping you company for a very long time." He turned away.

"No, stop!" Cedric ordered. "*Stop!*"

But he didn't stop. The guy sealed the door shut and left Cedric in that cell.

He yanked at the chains on his wrists. He bellowed.

Ella and Pate…Ella and Pate…

Rage built. Fury. Jealousy. Hate.

It built and built and…

Cedric began to smile.

***

His control was gone. Eric had stripped off his clothes as fast as he could. And Ella's—hers were on the floor.

They were still in Olivia's office. Ella was naked and spread out on that couch. Her eyes were open, so very blue, and locked on his. He could see her tiny fangs peeking out behind her plump, red lips.

His own fangs were out. And when she reached for him, he caught her wrist. He kissed her racing pulse and then he nipped her.

Her blood flowed on his tongue, driving up his lust even more. Making him wilder. So desperate for her.

He licked the small wound. Kissed it again. Then he parted her legs, opening her completely to him. Her light, tempting scent was making him drunk. His dick was so hard he felt like he'd erupt at any moment but—

He had to taste. *All* of her.

Eric put his mouth on Ella. On the sweetest spot. He licked and sucked and her moans filled his ears and just pushed his desperate need even higher. She came against his mouth. He felt her shudders and heard the cry of his name that broke from her lips.

It wasn't enough. He lifted up, positioned his cock, and when she locked her arms around him, he sank balls-deep into her.

Time froze. Her eyes were on him. So beautiful. *She* was beautiful. Perfect. The best thing in his life. That crystal clarity lasted an instant and then—

Take. Take. Take!

The beast in him took over. He drove faster. Harder. Deeper. They fell off that couch and hit the floor, but he took the impact. She straddled his hips, rising above him and surging down. Again and again. He heaved up. Caught her breast in his mouth. Laved the nipple. Sucked hard.

"Eric!"

He loved the way she said his name. Loved it even more when she screamed it.

But it wasn't enough. Madness drove him on. He flipped their positions so that he was on top again. He caught her legs. Pushed them over his shoulders. He could go into her even deeper now, and she moaned with each downward thrust of his hips as he stroked over her clit.

She was shaking. His heartbeat was drumming out of control.

He wanted to bite again. He wanted to fuck her endlessly.

He wanted to mark her. To own her.

To never, ever let go.

"Again!" Her voice was sharp as pleasure washed over her face. "Again, I'm coming—"

She was. Her sex squeezed him so tight.

Mark her. Own. Her.

Love?

Her.

He put his mouth on her shoulder. Bit down right in that spot where it curved toward her neck. Werewolves liked that spot.

He wasn't a werewolf.

But…*part* of him was.

And he wanted her.

He bit and thrust and he came, exploding within her on a wave of release so strong that the whole world went dark. He forgot everything else. Didn't care about anything else.

But Ella.

But the pleasure they shared.

They were in their own world. No fear. No pain.

Pleasure. Endless.

He started thrusting again. She was wet and hot and he slid deep into her. He always wanted to be with her. A part of her.

Again. Again.

He was hard once more. Swelling, thickening, as he slid into her hot channel. He couldn't get enough of her. Couldn't claim her deep enough. Couldn't touch her silken skin long enough. Couldn't hear her soft cries enough.

Nothing was ever going to be enough with her.

Forever wouldn't be fucking long enough.

***

"Help!"

Lawrence Carter tensed when he heard the cry. He'd been doing his sweep, checking on those in containment, and that weak cry barely reached him.

Cell unit eight. He headed closer, and opened the door with his security keycard. A quick glance assured him that the prisoner was still secure, the gold chains glinted. But the guy—he was on his knees. His head was bowed and the scent of burned flesh—a truly sickening scent—filled the air.

"The gold is too strong," the man said, gasping. "I-I can't…take more."

Lawrence lifted his radio. "I need assistance in unit eight. Bring the doc." Holly would know what to do for this guy. She always knew how to handle the paranormals.

The prisoner's head tilted back. Sure enough, there were burns on his throat. "A doctor…" He whispered. "Yes, that's what I-I need…"

Lawrence nodded. "One's coming."

"Get me…out of the chains…"

Did he look stupid? "That's not happening."

"They *burn*."

And without them, who the hell knew what the guy would do? "Pate wants you secured." *So you stay secured, buddy.*

"*Pate*." The word was said with such fury. "As much a monster as me…but he's not chained up, is he?"

At those words, Lawrence stiffened. "Pate's the one in charge here. The last thing that will ever happen is for him to get chained."

The prisoner's lips curled. "Don't be…so sure…"

Lawrence took a step toward him, but he made sure not to get close enough for the guy to touch him. He also held the fellow's collar remote in his hand.

"Never dealt with…someone like me…before…" The prisoner gasped out each word. "Don't understand…genetics…"

"Holly understands plenty about genetics." He knew the woman was flat-out brilliant. Scarily so sometimes.

"Take off...*collar.*" Now that sounded a whole lot more like an order, not a plea.

I don't take orders from prisoners. Lawrence's eyes narrowed. "That's not happening."

The fellow smiled at him. "I'll...remember you."

His guts were twisting. This scene was off. Sure, the guy was hurting, but he was also playing mind games. Lawrence's gaze shot to the video camera in the cell. He sure hoped the other agent on duty was watching this feed. Just in case, Lawrence lifted the radio to his mouth once again. "Get that back-up in here before the doc arrives—"

But there were footsteps behind him. He turned around and Holly was there. Her eyes were wide as she stared at the prisoner.

"Hurts..." The guy groaned.

Holly had a black medical bag with her. She shot a quick glance at Lawrence, then nodded when she saw the remote in his hand. "Keep him secure."

She hurried toward the prisoner.

And Lawrence just couldn't let her do it. The scene was *wrong.* The guy was acting weak, but his eyes were blazing. Lawrence jumped into Holly's path. "No, wait, don't—"

There was a *whoosh* of sound. The only warning he got. He looked over his shoulder and the prisoner's wings had stretched—*freaking grown even more*—and one wing flew out and slammed into Lawrence's back. Lawrence hurtled across the room and thudded into the wall. The remote fell from his fingers, sliding across the room. "Holly!" Lawrence yelled.

She leapt after the remote and grabbed it with a straining hand—

Just as the prisoner grabbed her. He lifted her into his arms.

Lawrence scrambled to pull out his gun. He'd tranq the bastard.

Holly was pressing the buttons on the remote but nothing was happening. The guy wasn't going down. He was laughing.

Lawrence aimed his weapon.

And the prisoner put Holly in front of him, using her as a shield. He wrapped one of his chains around her neck.

"Go ahead," the prisoner taunted. "Shoot. Bet I can snap her neck before I pass out."

Lawrence hesitated.

And in that moment, the jerkoff yanked up his left arm. The chain still encircled his wrist, but he'd yanked the other end of the chain straight out of the stone beneath him. The whole time…he'd been free?

"Just needed to get angry enough," the bastard whispered.

Then he whipped out that chain and slammed it into the side of Lawrence's head.

Holly's scream was the last sound Lawrence heard.

CHAPTER TWELVE

An alarm blasted, jerking Eric back to reality just when he was about to feast on Ella again. She was beneath him, her body around him, and he wanted to stay right the hell there.

But the alarm was blaring.

And…and someone was pounding at the door.

"Eric, dammit, we need you!" Olivia's yell. "Cedric has Holly!"

Cedric has Holly.

Eric pulled away from Ella and grabbed for his clothes. He yanked on his jeans and ran for the door. Pounding came again, and he nearly ripped that door right open.

Olivia stood on the other side, her face etched with fear.

"He has her in his cell," Olivia said as they started to race down the hallway. "I-I don't know what happened. He—"

"Someone needs to tranq the bastard."

"Lawrence is in there, too. He's hurt." A pause. "Badly."

Dammit! He turned to the right.

Then he whipped back around because the scent of lilacs was way, *way* too strong.

Ella was behind him. Face flushed, clothes a bit askew, eyes worried.

"No." Eric shook his head. "You stay in Olivia's office or go to our apartment. You *aren't* facing him."

"But—"

"I can't deal—shit, I have to know you're safe! I can't let him get close to you. I just *can't.*"

Her eyes glittered back at him. "And I can't stand by while he hurts someone else. And you promised, you *swore* you wouldn't lock me up again."

"Eric…" Olivia said, voice strained. "We don't have time to waste."

No, shit. Not with Lawrence hurt in there. Eric needed to go.

And I can't lock Ella up.

There wasn't a choice. "Don't get close to him," he ordered Ella. "And I do not like this shit!"

She nodded.

Then they were all running. Racing to containment unit eight. When he got there, guards were lined up outside. Not in. What the hell? He typed in his passcode and a live feed from the cell immediately appeared on the large screen to the left. He saw Lawrence—in a pool of blood. And Holly was there, with a golden chain wrapped around her neck.

If the guy broke her neck, Holly would recover. She was a vampire, after all. A little broken neck wouldn't stop her for long.

But…

Cedric had enhanced strength. Very, very enhanced…far more than Eric had anticipated. "He tore the chains right out of the floor." Sonofabitch. That floor had been made of the strongest material the government possessed. Supposedly paranormal proof.

Not.

If Cedric could rip the chains free, then he might not just be able to break her neck. In one swift move, he might be able to completely take her head.

There is no coming back from that.

Right then, Cedric's attention shifted and he stared straight at the small camera in his cell—so it appeared as if he were staring straight at Eric.

"Want to make a trade?" Cedric smiled and his fangs flashed. Now that Eric had accessed the feed to his cell, the audio system was easily picking up his voice. "Because I'm in the mood for a trade. You can take out the human…and *you* can come in, Eric."

Eric heard Ella's sharply indrawn breath.

"And you can come get *her…*" Cedric ran his hand down Holly's cheek. "You can get the doctor out, if you send in my Ella."

His gaze locked on her. *Hell, no.* Eric mouthed those words to her.

But Ella grabbed his arm. "He will kill her. He won't hesitate. Believe me, I've—I've seen just how brutal he can be."

And she thought he'd just let her waltz in there with the guy?

Eric hit the intercom button so that Cedric could hear what he had to say. "There is no way out of this place for you. There is no end game here."

"Don't worry about my games," Cedric threw back. "Do you want to trade?"

Trade… "No, I want to deal."

Cedric laughed.

"My agent is coming out, right now." Because Lawrence was bleeding too damn much. Eric had to get him out of there or the human would die. "And I'm going to come in. Just me."

"That's not the trade—"

"It's what you're getting." He shut off the intercom. Eric turned to the nearest guard and ordered, "Give me a gun loaded with wooden bullets. *Now.*"

The gun was immediately slapped in his hand.

He looked at the agents surrounding him. Connor watched, his face tense and his eyes starting to shine with power. Connor's brother Duncan was married to Holly. That meant this nightmare situation was real damn personal. "Is Duncan on the way?" Eric asked him. Duncan had been out on a different mission, but he knew Connor would have alerted the guy instantly.

"As fast as he can get here."

Good. "I'll take care of her." He couldn't let anyone see that fear had slipped through him. All of their lives, ever since they'd been kids, his job had been to protect his sister. Did Cedric realize how important she was? Did he know that he held all the power in his damn hands?

But I can't give him Ella. I won't.

"Whatever happens," Eric said flatly. "He doesn't leave this facility. I don't care what you have to fire at him. I don't care what you have to do...*he doesn't leave.*"

The agents nodded. And every man and woman there pulled out their weapons.

He turned for the cell door. His hand curled around the gun.

Ella stepped in front of him. "He has a plan. It's a simple one. You will die. He'll get out."

He flashed her a wide grin. "Have some faith, sweetheart." *I'm not Fey, but I'm not easy to kill either. He won't expect the pain I'll be bringing his way."*

"Eric—"

"And I'm sorry. I'm really fucking sorry but..." He motioned to Connor. "Keep her out here. He doesn't get near her, understand?"

Connor's hands settled around Ella's shoulders. "Yes, sir."

Fury darkened Ella's face. "No, you said—"

"I said I wouldn't lock you up. I never said I wouldn't put a guard on you." Then, voice lowering, he muttered, "I'll be damned if he gets his hands on two women I love."

"*What?*" Ella said. "What—"

But Eric straightened his shoulders. He kept his gun at his side and he headed into containment unit eight. He used his key card to open the door, and as soon as he stepped inside, the scent of Lawrence's blood filled his nostrils.

"So glad you joined my little party..." Cedric said. "But you forgot one very important guest."

"Ella isn't coming in here." He bent near Lawrence. The guy was still alive. Eric hoisted him up and glanced at Cedric.

Get the agent out.

Take care of Holly.

Kill Cedric.

He had a fairly simple plan in mind, too.

He'd tried containment. Tried to do things the right way. That hadn't worked. Now, he'd do things *his* way.

The chain was so tight around Holly's neck that she'd begun to bleed. Dark red streaks slid down her throat. She clawed at the chain, gasping, unable to speak.

"You need to loosen that hold," Eric told him flatly. "She can't breathe."

"Then I guess she'll suffocate. But we both know this one..." Cedric brought his head close to Holly's face and inhaled, "will take more than that to stay dead."

He does know that she's a vampire.

Lawrence groaned.

"You can take that one out," Cedric allowed with a shrug of his shoulders. "Humans don't interest me much these days."

Eric started to back toward the door.

Holly's eyes flashed wide and she tried to shake her head.

He stilled.

Cedric's gaze flickered over him.

Hell. "I'm guessing there's a bite mark somewhere on my agent. Beneath all of that blood. What did you do? Knock him out and then go in for a bite? You think I don't know how mind control shit works? I'll all too familiar with the power of a bite." He lowered Lawrence back to the floor. "Once he's clear of this room, what's supposed to happen? Will he turn on the others? Open the doors so you can fly away?"

Lawrence groaned. His eyelids fluttered open.

"Sorry," Eric said, "but that's not going to happen."

Holly was gasping. Struggling so desperately for breath.

He hated her pain. Rage and fear twisted through him.

"You're going to let your own man die?" Cedric demanded. His gaze jerked toward the camera once more. "Do you see him, Ella? Not such a hero now, is he? He's not—"

Eric lifted the gun and fired. The bullet slammed into Holly's chest and those terrible, desperate heaves stopped.

Her body shuddered. Her eyes closed.

"What the hell…?" Cedric's hold loosened on her for just a moment.

Vampires had a weakness. A stake to the heart—or, in this case, a wooden bullet—froze them. Quite literally. The vampire didn't breathe, didn't so much as twitch, until the bullet was removed.

Holly fell to the floor when Cedric's grip loosened on her.

And before the bastard could grab her again, Eric flew forward. He grabbed the guy, catching his still chained wrists and shoving them back against the wall. "You don't *fuck* with my team!"

Cedric heaved him away. Eric collided with the far wall, an impact hard enough to break his back.

If he'd been human.

"And you..." Cedric growled at him. "Don't *fuck* with my Ella!" He tossed out his chain and it flew straight for Eric's head. Just before impact, Eric shot to his feet. Then he motioned quickly with his hand and launched into another attack.

***

"That's the signal," Connor said as he kept a firm grip on Ella's shoulders. "Now get the hell in there and get our team out. But...tranq Lawrence. We can't take any risks with him."

The armed agents rushed inside. Ella tried to go after them. Connor just pulled her back. "Eric has this," he said, "and if you go in there, his attention will be shot to hell."

"He doesn't know what Cedric is capable of," Ella said. No one else did—*just me.*

"No, that bastard in there doesn't understand just what Eric Pate is capable of...but he's about to find out."

Eric was pounding his fist into Cedric's face. Hitting him again and again.

"That just makes him stronger," Ella said. "Pain and rage will give Cedric power."

The team had Lawrence. They dragged him out.

She watched as another agent reached for Holly.

Ella tensed.

But before that agent could get the doctor, Cedric's gold chains flew out again. The chains slammed into the man's back and he went down.

"Why the hell won't the guy's collar work?" Connor bellowed to the female agent standing at a nearby control panel. "Are we in the prisoner access system? Pump him full of gold!"

"We are!" The woman shouted back. "He won't go down. The collar—it has to be defective."

Ella couldn't take her eyes off the big screen that was giving her a perfect glimpse into Cedric's cell. "He broke the collar. The material it was made of—it wasn't strong enough. Just like the stones beneath him weren't strong enough to withstand his power."

They could press that remote function all day long, and nothing would happen.

"Get in there," Connor snapped to two more agents. "Fire tranqs at him until that guy goes down. He went down before. He'll go down again."

Cedric was trying to reach for Holly once more. He had his claws out and he was slicing down toward her neck.

"No!" Ella yelled.

Connor jerked toward the agents. "Hurry! Fire those tranqs! Now! Now!"

***

Eric's shoulder slammed into Cedric's stomach and he threw the SOB back as hard as he could.

Cedric just laughed as his wings brushed the ceiling. "That one…the doctor…she seems to matter more to you. Why is that? Did you fuck her, too?"

"Stay away from her." Eric put his body in front of Holly.

"Make me."

His fangs were burning in his mouth. The urge to rip and destroy had never been stronger for him.

Footsteps thudded in behind him. "Get her out!" Eric bellowed without looking back. Then he launched in for another attack.

But Cedric had been waiting, he was ready. He struck out hard, slicing right across Eric's chest.

Eric hissed at the pain, but he just slugged the bastard. Cedric roared and lunged toward Eric—

Gunfire. Blasts. The bullets tore into Cedric's body and he jerked, moving like a puppet on strings. Some of the bullets even sank into Eric, hitting his shoulder, his thigh. There was no way to avoid those hits because he was so close to the other man.

He ignored the pain.

Eric knew he was being hit with tranqs. They both were. Soon enough, Cedric would go down.

Or I will.

Cedric grabbed him. Eric locked his hands around the bastard's shoulders.

The gunfire halted.

"Keep firing!" Eric shouted. So they'd both get knocked out. He trusted his team. They'd drag his unconscious ass out of there. "*Fire!*"

The bullets hit him. Hit Cedric. The drugs poured through Eric's veins and he could feel his whole body growing sluggish.

But then…

Pain. Wrenching. Burning.

He shoved Cedric away and saw the fellow's blood-stained teeth.

"Now you're mine," Cedric whispered. His eyes were drooping closed. "I control…you…"

Bullshit. No one controlled him.

Eric's knees hit the floor. Cedric sagged right beside him.

"When you…you wake…" Cedric said. "Show Ella…show them all just what a monster…you really are…"

***

The agents carried Holly out of the room. Then three more men rushed in and dragged an unconscious Eric out. His head sagged forward and blood dripped from his neck.

Ella ran to Eric and when the agents tried to push her back, she snarled at them.

Her back began to burn. She could feel the stretch of her wings, just beneath the skin. Ella put her hand to Eric's throat. His pulse was there. Steady. Strong.

"He got tranq'ed, that's all," Connor assured her. "He'll wake up with one hell of a headache, but the guy *will* wake up."

Yes, he would. Her finger slid away from him.

Her gaze went to the door of containment unit eight.

"It's that bastard we have to worry about," Connor snapped. "Let's cover the guy with golden nets—we'll make sure he stays down."

Through the open door, Ella could see Cedric slumped on the floor. His wings were spread over his back.

"He isn't going to stay down," Ella said. "He's become too strong." She took a tranq gun from Connor. She went inside and stood over the man who'd tormented her for so long. Then she fired at him. Again and again until the gun just clicked. "But that will buy us a little more time."

And it had made her feel better, too.

She lifted her gaze from Cedric's prone form and found Connor staring at her.

"You have to tell me," he said flatly. "What weakness does he have?"

"Me."

Connor's gaze narrowed.

"I'm his weakness. And his wings—they're a weakness. Without wings, Fey lose so much of their power." She cleared her throat. "I have to see Eric. I-I need him." Just that—she needed to be with him. But she was afraid to leave Cedric, afraid he might attack again, and that fear must have shown on her face.

Connor's lips tightened. "We'll keep him sedated and secured. Don't worry. I'm personally gonna stand guard. The bastard won't be taking any more hostages."

She nodded and hurried away, rushing after the agents who were transporting Eric. They carried him into the med ward and put him on an exam table, one right beside Holly.

The other woman was far too still. Holly looked…dead.

Olivia was already in there, her face worried as she bent over Holly's body. She dug into Holly's chest and pulled that wooden bullet right out.

Flinching, Ella reached for Eric's hand. Her fingers curled around his. He felt so cold.

Olivia dropped the bullet into a small, shining tray and—

Holly's eyes flew open. Her breath rushed out. She shot upright and glanced around, her face confused and scared.

"It's all right," Olivia said quickly, soothingly. "You're safe."

Other agents were still gathered around the fallen human who'd been brought out of Cedric's cell. He was groaning a bit.

"You're totally safe," Olivia assured Holly. "Just—"

Holly leapt off the table. "Lawrence!"

"I checked his wounds," Olivia said quickly as she looked over at the human. "It looks bad, but he'll be—"

"Compulsion." Holly grabbed a syringe and drove it into Lawrence's neck.

Ella flinched. Wow. Someone was sure playing hard.

Eric's fingers squeezed hers.

"I-I heard Cedric give him the compulsion..." Holly's words stuttered out. "Cedric—he ordered him to k-kill all of us. Lawrence has to stay out until we can counter it."

Eric let out a groan.

Holly turned toward him. Blood soaked her shirt. "He shot me." Holly's lips trembled. "He does that too much, damn him." But the words were said without heat. And her eyes gleamed with tears. "He—"

Eric's grip turned painful on Ella's hand. Far too tight. She gasped and her gaze shot to his face. His eyes were open, but they were so hard—his gaze almost cruel.

Unease slid through her. "Eric?"

"Get…away…"

"Eric, you don't have to go anywhere. It's safe here. You're in the med ward. Everything's fine," she tried to reassure him.

He sat up. Should he have recovered that quickly? One minute he was out, the next he seemed completely, shockingly aware. He'd been pumped with a whole lot of tranqs. If he was already up…what about Cedric?

"In…my head…" Eric didn't let her go. He yanked her closer. "Get away…"

"Eric?"

"From me…" Eric growled.

Ella shook her head. He needed her. The last thing she wanted to do was leave him.

"Clear the room," Holly's sharp voice ordered. "Take Lawrence out of here. Olivia—stay with him. Everyone—*move.*"

But Ella couldn't move. Eric's grip on her was so strong and his eyes were so very tormented. Again, his gaze didn't seem just green but a wild mix of blue and green as he stared at her. His emotions were definitely out of control. She could *see* that.

"Don't...*hurt*..." Eric rasped.

"It's all right," she tried to soothe him once more. "Connor is guarding Cedric. You can trust him. You can—"

"*Cedric...*"

Eric's fangs were lengthening. And now his eyes were...darkening. The green and blue had nearly vanished completely. Fear skated up her spine.

"Ella, you need to leave," Holly said, her words strained. "You need to back away from him and leave right this minute."

She tried to pull away. He just tightened his hold even as he brokenly told her, "Go..."

She couldn't look away from him. "What's wrong with him?" Ella's question was for Holly.

"Was he bitten?" Judging by the way Holly asked that question, she already knew the answer.

"Yes." She'd seen that on the video feed. Cedric's teeth had torn into Eric's throat.

"If Cedric put Lawrence under a compulsion, it stands to reason he did the same thing to Eric."

"But Eric—he's part vampire!" *I tried to put him under a compulsion, and it didn't work.* So she'd thought any compulsion Cedric attempted to give wouldn't work either. "He resisted me, why can't he resist Cedric?" Why was this happening?

"Probably because we don't know just what the hell Cedric is! And maybe the guy is a lot stronger than you are, so his compulsions hold." Holly pulled harder on Ella. "Come on! I need you out of here. I need—"

Eric leapt off the exam table. He wrapped his arm around Ella, a steel band around her waist. "Go." He was still telling her to go but holding her so that she couldn't leave. *Eric's heart is saying one thing, but the compulsion is making him do another.*

Ella was facing Holly now. She saw the other woman's eyes flare wide.

Before Holly could speak, there was a sudden rush of pounding footsteps. Then a frantic roar of "*Holly!*" had the doctor's body jerking.

The doors burst open. A tall, dark-haired man stood there. He took one look at Holly and grabbed her, holding her desperately. "Blood, your blood," Ella heard him mutter. "*Your blood…*"

But Holly pushed him back. "Duncan, something's wrong with Eric."

Duncan's head shot up. His eyes—eerie, glowing eyes—locked on Eric…and Ella.

"Your claws are out, Eric," the man—Duncan—said softly. "And so are your fangs." Duncan stood at Holly's side. "Want to tell me what's going on?"

"Can't…hold on…long…"

"Can't hold on to what? The pretty woman in front of you?" Duncan's voice was flat. "Okay, then how about you let her go?"

"Never."

And then…something happened. Something changed with Eric—*in Eric?* – because he gave a deep, rumbling bellow—one that seemed to shake the very building behind her. His body began to shudder and twist. She tried to look back at him, but he held her too tightly. She didn't want to hurt him. Not Eric. Not—

He bit her. Sank his teeth into her neck and drank from her. Ella cried out because the bite was too rough. *He* was too rough. Not hurting her, but…close.

This isn't Eric.

Duncan streaked forward, grabbing out for her.

Eric lifted one hand and caught him around the throat. He didn't even seem to strain as he held him.

"I will kill you," Eric said to Duncan. His voice wasn't rasping any longer. It was cold and hard. "I will kill anyone in my way."

She couldn't let that happen. "Eric, *stop.*"

He just tossed Duncan aside, as if the man didn't matter.

Then he spun Ella to face him. His face—it had twisted. Contorted. Become far more savage. His eyes were so very dark now. And cold.

"I don't stop," he said. His smile flashed his fangs. "I do whatever I want. I can kill, I can take, and *there will be no stopping me.*"

Fear grew within her, but she fought it back. "Holly, you and Duncan get out of here. Keep the doors barred. Don't let anyone else inside."

"And what's supposed to happen to you?" Holly yelled back.

"*She stays,*" Eric snarled.

"I stay," Ella said, her voice soft. "Go find a way to break the compulsion." Just putting him under with a tranq wasn't going to do it. He would recover too fast and just come at them again. They had to get Eric back. *Her* Eric. Not this stranger.

I have to get him back.

"He won't hurt me," Ella said even as her neck throbbed. *Liar, liar.* "Just go!" She held her breath until she heard the door close behind her.

Eric stared down at her. She thought he was going to try and bite her again but then he cried out, as if in pain.

He pushed her away.

And he hit the floor, slamming down to land on his hands and knees.

"Eric?"

"No control…not anymore." His bones were snapping. Popping. "Beast…coming out."

She started to retreat toward the door. Then Ella stopped. They were in this together. They had a deal. No, no, they had a whole lot more than that.

"You're shifting," she said.

His shoulders stretched. His claws lengthened. His back—it looked as if something were trying to tear right through his back, along the ridges of his shoulder blades.

Wings? No, of course not, not possible but…

Eric had told her he was the blend of many creatures. Powerful paranormal creatures. If his control was truly gone…if he were following Cedric's dark orders, then she couldn't let him out of that room. He could be a threat to everyone in the building.

While he was on the floor, changing, shifting before her, she ran and grabbed a silver collar that had been left out on the shelf. A remote was right next to it. She jumped back to Eric and locked that collar in place as fast as she could.

He had werewolf blood in him. So maybe the collar would keep him in check. Maybe.

"I'm sorry, Eric," she said and she pressed the button on the remote.

He stilled.

Her breath heaved out. The silver was working. Good. *Good.* Now they could calm down and come up with a plan to—

His long, claw-tipped fingers yanked that collar right off. It literally fell apart beneath his hands. Then he rose before her. He rose and behind Eric, she saw the dark shadows that *shouldn't* be there.

But those shadows grew. His growls filled the air as he kept changing. The shadows deepened and a quiet rustle filled the air.

Every bit of moisture vanished from Ella's mouth. "So I guess I was…kind of right after all." His wings stretched toward the ceiling. *Wings.* "Were you holding back on me?"

His gaze burned with dark fire. *"Mine."* Then he flew straight at her.

His hands locked around Ella and she didn't even have the chance to scream, not before he'd whirled them around and flown straight out of the window. Good thing they were on an upper floor—otherwise, she got the feeling he might have just burst right through the ceiling and destroyed that whole place as he fought for freedom.

But the glass shattered. They escaped. Eric hurtled away into the night, and Ella held onto him with all of her might.

***

"What. The. Fuck?" Duncan McGuire stared at the broken window. "What happened here?"

Holly peered into the night. They'd gone rushing in to the med ward when they heard the breaking glass. Now she could see the distant figure. One moving far too fast.

"Eric has wings," she whispered. *How does Eric have wings?*

Duncan caught her hand. "Holly, baby..." He cleared his throat. "Mind telling me just when your brother sprouted wings?"

"I'm guessing about two minutes ago." But she would be finding out exactly what had happened to him. She'd pour over the recent bloodwork she'd done on him. She'd help her brother—get him back.

"How?"

Now Eric was just a tiny dot in the distance. But he was a dot she could track. "I have no idea." She'd have to attack that problem later. Right now, she needed to get Eric and Ella back to the base. She exhaled slowly as she fought to maintain her calm. *Eric seriously just flew out of here.* "Let's get a team and go after them. Eric Pate out of control—shifting like he is—he's a threat that we can't allow loose in the city." They'd have to stop him.

One way or another.

***

Connor glared at Cedric's prone form. They'd put three gold collars on the bastard while he was knocked out, just to be extra careful. And they'd moved his ass to another maximum security containment area. New chains were on his wrists and his ankles.

Connor had just been informed about the chaos in the med ward. About Eric's freaking *flight*. He wanted to rush out with Holly and Duncan and help retrieve the director, but he also didn't want to leave Cedric alone with the humans. He knew Eric would want him to stand guard, and after Cedric's last attack…

I can't risk him putting compulsions on anyone else. So Connor crossed his arms over his chest and waited. The guy would wake up, sooner or later.

And when he did, the compulsion that Cedric must have placed on Eric…it would be ending. Connor would make sure of it, even if he had to kill the guy in order for it to vanish.

CHAPTER THIRTEEN

They landed in a dark alley. The moonlight shone down on them. The beat of music drifted in the air. Ella could hear people's voices floating on the wind, and the idea that humans were so close terrified her.

Eric's wings folded down, seeming to vanish behind him.

He stood in front of her now, maybe two feet away, and he just—stared at her.

"Eric?" Ella managed. "Please tell me that you know me. That you've got some control still inside." *Please.*

"I'll kill for you." Again, he spoke in that odd, cold voice. The one that she hated because it didn't sound like her Eric talking. More like a stranger.

Ella shook her head. Those humans were definitely too close, and, judging by the voices, they were getting closer with every moment that passed. "I don't want you to kill for me."

"I'll make them scream. And bleed." He turned and headed for the street.

She raced after him and managed to jump in front of him, stopping him with a hard jab to the chest. "No! I don't want anyone screaming. Or-or bleeding!" She shook him. Tried to, anyway. He didn't exactly shake much. "This isn't you. I want *you* back."

"I am back. Now." And his wings rose behind him. "I'm just what you wanted. The mate who was waiting for you."

"You weren't Fey before," she whispered. "You said you weren't." But all along, hadn't she been responding to him as if he were? Then he'd told her she was wrong. *I wasn't the wrong one.*

He smiled. A flash of white in the dark. "I'm many things. All things. The worst of the monsters. The strongest. They're all in me. I'm the beast everyone should fear. I'm the one who will wreck them all."

"No, you aren't. You're a good man, Eric. You're a protector. *That's* who you are."

But footsteps were coming toward them. Drunken laughter. She looked over her shoulder and saw two men staggering their way.

One guy caught sight of her and gave a long, high whistle as he hurried away from his friend. "Hellooo, pretty lady!" He called out as his voice slurred. "Are you looking for a good time? Cause I can show you—"

Eric had him. In a blink, he'd eliminated the distance between himself and his prey. Eric locked a hand around the guy's neck and jerked him forward. Then Eric sank his teeth into the man.

"No!" Ella yelled as the human screamed. She grabbed at Eric, and when he wouldn't stop, when he wouldn't let the fellow go, she drew back her hand to punch him and—

Gunfire.

It blasted, hitting hard. Hitting…her. Ella felt the warmth of her blood pouring down her shirt. She looked down, saw the dark stain on her shirt, and then her gaze snapped to the mouth of the alley.

The other human stood there. Still swaying drunkenly, only now he had a gun in his hand. He must have been carrying that gun all along. *Humans can be dangerous.* "L-let my buddy go, f-freak!" He yelled. He fired again.

The second bullet didn't hit Ella.

Because Eric had already attacked. He'd grabbed the shooter. Broken his arm with a quick, vicious yank, and Eric slammed his fist into the man's face. There was the crunch of more bones and Ella knew the human's nose was broken.

"You don't touch mine!" Eric's roar was almost deafening. "You don't hurt…*mine.*"

Ella put her hand to her chest and staggered forward. "Stop this!" Ella yelled at him.

There was a *whoop, whoop, whoop* overhead.

She didn't look up.

"Eric, stop!"

He was pummeling the guy.

"I'm okay!" She used a burst of her speed and managed to tear the human from Eric's arms. And Eric's fist froze mid-motion, right above her.

Her breath heaved out. Staring into his eyes right then, she didn't see much of the man she'd known at all. He was feral. So wild. So...

Dangerous.

She could fight him, but that might stir up his beast even more.

Or she could try to reach the man inside. The man she'd thought was her mate from the beginning. The man. Not the beast.

Not *any* of the beasts that her lover carried. Werewolf. Vampire. Fey.

No wonder control was such an issue for him.

When he let go, he really did turn wild.

Ella tilted her neck to the side, offering her throat to him. "I don't think you're going to hurt me," she said.

His fist lowered. Opened. Then his fingers were reaching out to touch her throat.

The *whoop, whoop, whoop* was even louder now, but Eric didn't look away from her.

"Don't be so sure of that," he told her. "There are so many things I want to do with you. To you..."

"You have wings." It seemed important. "I didn't think you were Fey."

His smile was cold. She almost wished she couldn't see so well in the dark. "Guess the government spliced my DNA with everything they had."

And what—he'd just needed to be pushed hard enough for that part of him to emerge?

His claws were on her throat. A werewolf's claws. His fangs were bared. Vampire fangs. And his wings were out—a Fey's wings. What else was there? What else lived inside of Eric? Did she even want to know?

"And you thought you were the evil one," Eric whispered. "I'll show you how evil I can be."

His mouth was right over her throat. To rip it open—

Or to kiss her?

"You won't," Ella said. Her eyes drifted closed. Her hands curled around his shoulders. Massive shoulders. He hadn't done a full-on shift, but he'd sure gotten one hell of a lot bigger. "I trust you."

"*You shouldn't.*" His hand fisted in her hair. He pulled her head back even more, exposing her neck fully.

Ella smiled. "Go ahead…show me just how bad you really are. But I know you won't hurt me." It was easier to say without looking into his eyes. Without seeing him. "We had a deal, you and me. An agreement."

Whoop, whoop.

His breath blew over her throat. She waited.

Teeth. Fangs.

Or a kiss?

Her heart raced too fast. Her claws dug into his arms and he—

He kissed her. A light, soft kiss on her neck.

"You smell…" Eric muttered. "Like you're…mine." His voice wasn't so cold now. More strangled. Confused. "No, you smell…"

Ella's eyes opened.

"Lilacs. Paradise." Eric seemed to force out the words. "Every dream…everything I want…"

He was coming back to her.

And just in time. A rough blast of wind blew her hair and she looked over her shoulder, back into the street, and she saw that a helicopter had landed just beyond the entrance to the alley. Para Agents were rushing forward, with their guns up.

There had better just be tranqs in those guns. Surely they wouldn't shoot to kill their own director?

If the director had claws and fangs and wings…maybe.

And Eric was back to snarling and growling because he'd finally noticed them. He pushed her behind his body and his wings spread wide, shielding her totally as she screamed for him to—

"Stop!"

He didn't. He flew forward. The guns blasted.

Two agents went down.

A third.

More bullets came at Eric.

In a flash, a fourth and fifth agent were groaning on the ground, bleeding from Eric's claws.

And…Holly was there. Standing near the helicopter. Lifting a gun and pointing it straight at Eric. Duncan was at her side.

They were the only two Para Agents still standing.

Ella rushed toward them, running in a quick burst of her supernatural speed.

But Holly fired. And finally, finally Eric staggered. He dropped to his knees before his sister.

"I guess it was my turn to shoot," Holly murmured.

Eric's body slammed forward onto the cement. Ella reached him an instant later. She flipped him over, frantic. He was still breathing. His eyes were closed.

"We need to get him back to the base," Duncan ordered the scattered group of agents. "And get him contained."

Contained.

"Now," Duncan barked to the agents who were trying to rise. "And somebody…go tell the humans there's a gas leak in that bar. That they're having delusions. No winged man was out here."

Eric was going to be contained. If he couldn't be brought back to his senses, what then?

He was strapped to a gurney. A collar was put around his neck—no, *two* collars were locked around him.

"One is silver," Holly explained. "And one has liquid gold inside. He won't be getting away from us again."

But…

He shouldn't be caged. It wasn't Eric's fault. Cedric had done this to him. Cedric had pushed him to let the beast out.

And if Cedric didn't *un*do the compulsion…*Eric can't be contained forever.* She wouldn't let that happen to him.

***

Cedric's eyes slowly opened. He blinked blearily, and Connor waited for the asshole to focus on him. He stood about ten feet from Cedric. Well away from the chains and the guy's wingspan.

Slowly, Cedric pushed up. He groaned and his hand immediately went to his collar—*collars.*

"Get these damn things off me!" Cedric shouted.

"Not happening." Connor kept his voice flat.

Cedric squinted as he stared at him. "You…am I supposed to be scared of you?"

"You should be scared of a whole lot of things. But, yeah, I am one of those things."

Cedric laughed. "I don't have to fear anyone or anything."

We'll see about that. "You put a compulsion on two good men today. Take that compulsion off them."

"No."

"That's not the right answer." He pointed toward the ceiling. A net made of gold hung above Cedric. "How about we try that again?"

Cedric swallowed, then said, "I can't undo it. They're stuck. Stuck like that until death."

"You'd better be talking about *your* death," Connor warned him. "Because someone will be dying soon, only it won't be them."

***

"He's sedated and restrained." Holly's voice was quiet. Almost clinical. Actually, it *was* clinical. And Ella didn't think it should have been. Not when the woman was talking about her own brother. "He isn't a threat to anyone now."

Ella stared through the observation glass. Eric was strapped down on a table in the other room. His eyes were closed and his breathing was shallow.

"Do you want me to patch up your wounds?" Holly asked.

"No, they're fine." Already healing. She moved closer to the glass. "What's going to happen?"

"Connor and Duncan will find a way to eliminate the compulsion on him. He'll be back to normal soon."

"Will he?" How did you go back once the beast was free? "Did you know…just what he was?"

"Did I know he'd let himself become some kind of walking science experiment for the government?" Now that clinical quality fractured in her voice. "Hell, no. But now I understand why he kept pushing me to find a cure for vampirism. For the werewolf bite. Maybe…I think he wanted to go back. To undo what he'd become."

She didn't see his wings. Had he already shifted so that they were hidden once more? "I mean about him being Fey." She *had* been right before when she sensed he was like her. And now she was all confused. Was her response to him based on the mating instinct? Or was it deeper? Something even more primal?

Something like…love.

No, no, love is dangerous. Love will make me weak. It wrecked my world before.

When she'd given her heart to the wrong man. A man who was still destroying those close to her.

"I had no idea," Holly said and Ella believed her. "I don't even know where he'd get the material for a change like that or *how* he'd do it."

She had a suspicion. "Maybe someone in your government has been collecting Fey wings. And using them to make new monsters." Now she was sad. "We're kind of like butterflies. If you cut off our wings, we die."

Holly sucked in a sharp breath. "Ella, I'm sure that Eric *didn't* – "

"How did you track us so fast?" That question had been nagging at her. "Don't get me wrong. It was great to see the cavalry arrive, but I don't quite understand how you found us so quickly." She glanced over at Holly. "Or how Eric found me at that church."

Holly's gaze cut away from hers.

"I would really like the truth."

Holly gave a faint nod. "You…you have a tracking device. Embedded beneath the skin of your hand. I put it there…when you got cut trying to escape."

Her heart seemed to slow. "Eric wanted it there."

"He was trying to protect you!"

Sadly, Ella glanced back through the glass. "No, I think he was just trying to track me. I know what it's like to be hunted." But she hadn't realized, not until then, that Eric was the one hunting her. Her hand lifted and touched the glass. "So close," Ella whispered. "I thought I nearly had what I wanted..."

***

"So..." Connor drawled as he studied the prisoner. "You injected yourself with everything you could find...and you made yourself into what—a Fey wannabe? A distorted version of a real beast?"

Cedric just laughed. "Isn't that what Eric Pate did? What *you* did? Nature didn't make you strong enough, so you had to take evolution in your own hands, just like me."

The bastard sure wasn't acting weak. Were all the tranqs already out of his system? Talk about a fast metabolism rate.

"But one disadvantage you have...I'm smarter than you are," Cedric said, smirking. "So much smarter. And I've been around for a hell of a lot longer."

"Get rid of the compulsion on Eric and Lawrence."

"No," Cedric said. Then he laughed. "Do you know...I still remember the first time I realized I could work a compulsion—I had a young Fey in my dungeon. I got him to cut off his own wings. Amazing, really…that was when I knew my experiments had worked. I could control anyone or anything—*I* had that power. And I was going to use it."

"You're a sick freak, you know that?" Disgust twisted his lips.

Cedric just laughed. "I'm not the only freak in the place. Your *director*, Eric Pate. I could smell all the beasts just waiting to spring out of him. Perhaps he shouldn't have fought his true self for so long. Maybe he shouldn't have taken all those drugs that he did to keep his control in place…maybe *then* he would have been able to fight me." He shrugged. "But maybe not. Maybe nothing would have changed his fate. Now he's mine. Mine to use and then mine to kill."

Connor glared at the bastard. "There's an easy way to end this." His claws shot out. "I can just kill you now and we're all be home free."

Cedric's eyes were slits. "I'm sure you would like to think so, but the truth is, I didn't come in here, flying blind. I came to this place to get my Ella back."

"I don't think she considers herself to be yours."

Actual sadness seemed to flash across the guy's gaze. "I have lived a long time," he murmured. "Long enough that I developed powers others didn't. After all, I created the first vampires…with my lovely brew. I made them. I made werewolves. I made all those beasts out there. So it really only stands to reason that I control them. No matter how far away from me they are."

"Keep up the lies," Connor told him. "They'll just—"

"Kill her, Eric."

Ice slid down his spine. "What did you just say?"

Cedric smiled. "I gave another compulsion. I can do that, you see. Once my bite is there, the prey doesn't have to be close anymore. It's almost like I poison them…poison their minds so that they can only hear me."

"Then who the hell did you just order him to kill?"

"Ella." He laughed. "All those centuries, looking for her, and she betrayed me. Did you think I'd let that happen? No…not ever. He'll try to kill her, and you see, she'll have to fight back against him. She'll fight him and in the end…" Again, that twisted laughter slid from him before Cedric said, "I'm betting on her. She's the real Fey. They always fight to the death. Then Eric will be no more, and Ella will have learned a very valuable lesson."

He's bullshitting. He has to be— "What lesson is that?" Connor demanded.

"You don't screw around on *me*."

Connor stared into his eyes. The bastard wasn't bullshitting.

"I'm killing you," Connor said. "*That* will stop it. That will end—"

"End her? Yes, yes it would." His eyes gleamed. "Do you know why I kept searching for her, all these years? These long endless years? Because we were linked. I did that. I made it so. Bound us so tightly together. She wouldn't be with another, no matter what she thought. Ella would always be tied…with me. To me."

"That's not possible."

"*Anything* is possible," Cedric snarled right back. "When I had her in my dungeon, I knew I couldn't live without her. So I made certain she couldn't live without me. I die, she dies." When he talked of Ella, his face showed a wild mix of longing and hate. "Fitting, isn't it? Either one of her lovers will kill her…the big, tough FBI agent who was supposed to save the world or…" His eyes were icy. "Or she'll die when one of you dumbasses decide it's time for me to go to hell. The instant that you kill me, Ella is dead, too. She doesn't win. She doesn't escape, and *she doesn't live without me!*"

Sonofabitch…the guy was crazy. Crazy as all hell. But…

Connor whirled for the door, roaring for the guards outside. *I also think the bastard is telling the truth.*

***

He was being watched.

Eric lay on the table, heavy metal straps cutting into his skin. Someone had strapped him down to that table. Silver straps. Like that was supposed to do something to him. Holly should have known better.

All of the strengths. None of the weaknesses. He was a true cross-over.

The silver wouldn't hurt him. But it did annoy him. Holly should have been more careful. Holly…*my sister*…He could see her in his mind—her hair pulled back, her delicate features worried—

The thought, the image that had been there vanished.

What the hell is happening? What is wrong with me?

He kept his eyes closed. He didn't want to give anything away to the watcher. He could feel the eyes on him, and Eric tried to figure out what was going on around him.

His mind seemed splintered. When he attempted to grab a thought, a memory of the last few hours, things got hazy.

Rage was in his mind. A fury that felt as if it belonged more to an animal than a man. And he was a man…wasn't he?

He tried to push past that rage.

He heard a faint squeak. Caught the soft pad of a footstep. Smelled lilacs.

"Are you going to continue pretending that you're still out?" Her voice was soft and sensual, and it stroked right over him.

For an instant, the rage flared even hotter within him. *No one can take her. Need her. Kill…for her.*

"I know you're awake. I saw your breathing change. Holly told me I was crazy to come inside, but I think I can reach you. Or maybe I just hope that I can."

His eyes opened. His head turned, and Eric saw her. A wild tangle of dark hair. Eyes that saw too deep. Red lips.

And a smile that…seemed to break something in him. *Her smile shouldn't be sad. I don't want her sad.*

"Guess what I just found out? You put a tracking device on me." Her lips thinned. "Completely not cool, Eric. Very stalker-like, and *not* part of our deal."

Deal.

You couldn't make a deal with the devil. *Is that what I am?*

She crept closer. The scent of lilacs deepened. He liked that scent.

"Did you know, all along, that you had Fey DNA in you? That your wings would come out if you just let go of that precious control and your wild side took over?"

He didn't have wings. Wait…a quick flash pushed through his mind. Him, holding the beautiful woman right beside him. Flying.

Sonofabitch.

"What…" The one word was more growl than anything else as he forced himself to speak. "Happened?" More images and memories pushed through his mind. Splinters…

"You're under a compulsion. Probably some bull about letting your beast out and control just being a memory for you. I don't know exactly what Cedric said to you—"

Cedric.

And he could see the bastard. Smirking. Blood around him. Gold chains…

Show them all just what a monster…you really are…

Eric roared and shoved upward. The bars restraining him groaned. Bent. Broke.

He jumped to his feet and stood there, his chest heaving, his fangs burning, and his claws most definitely out.

She didn't retreat. She should have. She took a step closer. "I figured those wouldn't really hold you for long." Her hand lifted and he saw the gun she held. "I think I'm supposed to pump you full of tranq, but I don't want to do that."

Bad plan. I'll have that gun out of your hand before you can fire the first shot.

"Do you know who I am?"

Absolutely. Even through the rage and pain and madness that was his mind, he recognized her. "Mine."

Her lips curled and her half-smile made his chest ache even more. "It's not like my name is 'Mine,' you know. I'm a person. Not a thing you own."

He wanted to own her. Possess her. Claim her.

Love her?

Eric shook his head. Hard.

"Come on," she urged him. "Say my name. You can do it. You know me."

He did. "El…la…" Again. Speech was way too hard. Because a beast didn't speak.

And her smile stretched. Her eyes lit up. A real smile. That ache he felt got worse. *Something is very wrong with me.*

"That's right. I'm Ella. And you're Eric. You're the director of the Para Unit. Do you remember the Para Unit?"

Vampires. Werewolves. Humans. Hell.

He nodded. His breathing rasped out. Every instinct he had screamed that he should attack—but attack what? Who?

Not her. Not ever her.

"And Purgatory? Do you remember Purgatory?"

A flash came in his mind again. A prison, surrounded by the rough waves of an ocean. Silver bars. Drugged vampires. Once more, he managed a grim nod.

Her shoulders sagged. "Good. We're making progress." Then she stepped even closer to him. Her right hand lifted and pressed to his bare chest, right over his heart. He felt her touch, burning right through him. Sliding beneath his skin. Straight to his soul.

I don't have one.

Did he?

"If you can't come back to me, if you keep attacking your own men, they will try to send you to Purgatory. They'll think you broke. That the beast won." Her smile was gone now. "I won't let that happen to you. I'll do anything to save you."

Why? He couldn't force that word out.

Desire burned in him. Her touch had ignited a firestorm. His cock ached and he wanted to lift her up, spread her legs, and fuck her deep and hard. Right there.

He wanted to bite her and mark her.

He wanted to keep her.

Love...Again, that one word whispered through him.

But...

"Eric?" She rose onto her tip-toes, standing before him, seemingly completely unaware of the danger right in front of her. "Please, I need you to talk to me. I need you to come back to me."

His hand lifted and his claws trailed over her arm. It would be so easy to attack.

A beast would attack.

Not her.

She shivered. "I can go to Cedric. I can offer him a deal. I can—"

He yanked her up, spun around and put her down on that exam table, caging her with his arms and his legs.

Ella gulped and peered up at him through her lashes. "That was fast. I'm guessing the tranqs aren't in your system now? Super-fast metabolism," she muttered. "Super-fast."

"Fuck."

Her brows shot up. "Uh, Eric—"

He kissed her. Too rough. Too hard. Too deep. Her hands rose up and pushed against his chest. She was trying to stop him.

Because I'm wrong. I'm...beast?

He nipped her lower lip, and she gasped. Her lips parted more and he drove his tongue inside.

His cock was so full and thick, and being in her—he *had* to get inside of her.

But she turned her head away. "Eric, I don't—"

"*Help.*" Speaking was so damn hard. He needed her to understand. Something was rising in him. He could feel it. The muscles in his back were aching. The bones seeming to bend. He was changing and he couldn't stop it.

But in his mind, he'd remembered a time when he'd felt in utter control—of every part of himself. When he'd felt… "Peace," Eric rasped.

She stilled.

He'd been at peace when he'd been in her. With her. Then all his demons had quieted. It had been the best moment of his life.

With her.

Her eyes searched his. "I think I'm getting this…" She tossed her shirt aside, baring her breasts to him. Small but round, with beautiful, dark tips. "Just to be clear…I want you. I always have, and I think I always will."

He took her breast in his mouth. Tasted her. And the madness in his mind quieted, just for a moment.

Not a beast. A man. That's what she does. She—

He felt the wings break through his back. Ella gasped and stiffened in his arms.

He stepped back, just far enough to yank off her jeans. His claws pretty much shredded her panties, but he didn't touch her skin. He couldn't hurt her.

Ella was special.

Ella was…

Everything.

"Your wings are beautiful," she told him.

And she was staring at him with awe in her eyes. There was no fear there. No doubt. She trusted him so completely.

When he didn't trust himself.

"S-sorry…" For all he'd done. For—

"Shut up and kiss me," Ella told him. "And then fuck me. Hard and wild. The way we both like."

No, she wasn't afraid. She wanted him—every bit of him. And she was fighting to keep him with her. Fighting the darkness and the madness. She'd said that she would do anything to bring him back.

And he would do anything to stay with her.

His mouth took hers. Deep and wild. Her taste pushed through his madness and just drove up his desire. A lust that was taking over everything else.

If he didn't have her right then, he was afraid to see what he'd do.

What I'll become.

Because Ella was his peace. She was his hope.

He made sure nothing was between them. He touched her, flesh to flesh. He reached down to position his cock—

"I've got this," Ella whispered. Her smooth, soft fingers stroked him, pushing him closer and closer to the edge. A veil of red covered his vision.

He could feel the silky, creamy opening of her sex waiting for him. Paradise, right there. Worth killing for. Worth dying for.

Worth living for.

Eric drove into her, and there was no going back. No restraint left, not once that white-hot channel closed around him. Deeper, harder. Faster. He sank into her again and again. He bit her neck, savored her blood on his tongue, and had to take more—all. All she'd give him.

He yanked her off the table. Her legs wrapped around him and he lifted her up, again and again and again. She braced herself by locking her hands around his shoulders. Her gaze met his—so fucking beautiful.

He saw himself in her eyes.

Saw—

Ella cried out as a climax hit her. He felt the contractions of her release around him and he shattered. He forgot everything else in his blind drive. The room seemed to whirl around them. Was he flying? He didn't know. Didn't really care. He was in her, balls-deep, and he was coming, riding out a wave of release that hollowed him out. That took everything—

In that one instant, he knew he wasn't a beast. But he wasn't a man.

He was both.

Eric's wings folded. He collapsed on the floor, dragging Ella down with him as his mind shut down—as all the rage and fear and hate left him.

There was only peace.

Only Ella.

***

"Okay, do we go in?" Duncan asked carefully. "It's too damn quiet in there, and I'm afraid he might have killed her."

She could tell he was half-serious. There had been plenty of noise before in there. It had sounded as if the whole room was being destroyed.

There had even been a few screams.

And it had been awkward. Very awkward. It was such a good thing she'd shut the blinds on that observation window. Holly cleared her throat. "Let's just give Ella a little bit longer to, uh, work her charm on him, okay?"

"You're saying she isn't dead." Duncan's hands were on her shoulders. Carefully massaging her.

"She's not dead," Holly was definite on that. But—

Footsteps thundered behind her. She looked over her shoulder and saw Connor rushing toward her.

"Problem," he gritted out. "Big damn problem."

Duncan swore. "Let me guess…that dick Cedric?" His fangs flashed. "I'll be happy to handle that bastard after what he did to Holly."

But Connor was glancing frantically around the area. "He just sent out another compulsion. Apparently, once he has his victim's blood, he can always control them. And he—he just ordered Eric to kill Ella."

Holly staggered back. Then she ran for the door of the med ward.

"Where is Ella?" Connor demanded. "Where is she?"

"She's with him!" Holly yelled and she fumbled to open that damn door.

CHAPTER FOURTEEN

They were on the floor. Ella's heartbeat drummed frantically in her chest. They'd been flying at some point. She was pretty sure of that. But her wings weren't out, so they'd been moving purely under Eric's steam.

His wings were still there, beautiful and big and she roused enough to touch one, inhaling sharply when she felt the soft silk of his wing beneath her fingertips.

Then her gaze looked past his wing. They'd…wrecked that lab. Tables were overturned. Medical instruments scattered across the floor.

So things had gotten a little intense.

She cleared her throat and looked back down at Eric. She was currently straddling him. He was in her. And his gaze—*totally focused on me.*

Ella smiled at him. "I don't know if that helped you, but it seriously helped me."

"Ella!"

The door flew open. Holly stood in the doorway. Her face looked absolutely horrified.

Right. Because I'm naked and on top of her step-brother. This is the stuff of nightmares.

Frantic, she tried to rise.

But Eric's hands flew up.

His hands curled around—around her throat.

Connor and Duncan both burst into the room. As if things couldn't get any more embarrassing for her.

"Privacy," Ella said. "A moment of—" She broke off because Eric's hands had seemed to tighten on her throat.

"Let her go," Connor barked. "Come on, man, do it now."

Eric's jaw had clenched. His eyes shone with emotion. As if he were fighting. Struggling.

She waited.

"Uh, Ella, you may need to kick his ass," Connor said. "Not that we all haven't thought of doing it a time or twenty…"

She ignored him. "I love you, Eric."

His fingers feathered over her throat.

"And I trust you."

His breath heaved out. He shot up, moving so that they were now facing each other, their bodies brushing.

"*Love…you…*" Eric rasped to her.

"That's great, fabulous," Connor snarled. "But Ella, you're not getting that he's under a compulsion to—"

Eric kissed her. Sweetly. Softly. And his fingers were lightly caressing her jaw.

"You are my peace," Eric whispered to her.

And he was hers.

"Um, he's not attacking her," Holly said.

Ella wrapped her arms around him. Held him tight.

"He's under a compulsion," Connor said again. "Cedric ordered him to kill you, Ella."

"He's not going to kill me." She'd never thought he would. "He can't."

Eric shuddered against her. "Hell, *no*. Never."

Because she'd reached him. Or maybe…maybe she'd never lost him.

"Okay, I'm going to need you to both put on clothes so that my eyes stop burning," Connor said. "Then we have some serious shit to discuss. Because this mess isn't over. Not by a long shot."

"No," Eric's voice was coming easier. Sounding far more human as he pushed his beast—beasts?—back. "It's not. It won't be over…until I end Cedric."

Silence.

"Don't plan on doing that just yet," Connor finally said. "Because there are some things you need to know first."

***

She'd saved him. Brought him out of the chaos of his beast and his shift and she'd given him hope. Ella stood by Eric's side, dressed now—both of them were so that Connor's eyes would stop burning—and her fingers were wrapped around his. He couldn't stop touching her. Didn't want to stop. She was his link to sanity, and Eric rather thought that she always would be.

"So is the compulsion gone?" Holly asked as she paced near him.

"I don't feel him," Eric told her quietly. "And I also don't feel the urge to destroy everything around me."

"Yeah, we're all glad you aren't hulking out anymore," Connor supplied, "but what was with the wings? You took Fey DNA and you didn't tell us?"

He shook his head. And he hated to say this. "I don't know." He stared into Ella's eyes because she deserved this from him. She deserved a million things. "I volunteered for every experiment that Uncle Sam offered up to me. I didn't ask where they had gotten the serums, not back in those days. Vampires had attacked my whole team—I'd seen werewolves decimate families. I wanted to help. I wanted to be strong enough to fight back, and I didn't think past the moment. I had *no* idea that the government had Fey or that—"

"I don't think they did," Holly said.

All eyes turned to her.

Some of her hair had come loose from her braid, and she tucked a lock behind her ear. "I spent some time looking at your test results again, Eric. Remember when I was so afraid her blood would kill you? And I—"

"Poked and prodded me with your needles? Yeah, I remember."

Holly cleared her throat. "I got the results back when you were—um, occupied with Ella. Her blood isn't killing you. Quite the opposite. It appears to have…been a trigger."

He wasn't following. "A trigger?"

"You know how only some people can become werewolves? Those who already have altered DNA? When humans are bitten by werewolves, two things happen…they die or they transform." Her breath sighed out. "Your DNA was different. When she bit you…when you bit her and the blood exchanged…there was a trigger. What had been dormant within you, well, it wasn't any longer."

He shook his head even as he felt Ella's fingers tense around his. "You're saying…I was always Fey?"

"*Dormant* Fey. Somewhere back in your blood line, I'm guessing you had an ancestor who was Fey and that ancestor produced a child with a human."

His mother had died when he'd been so young. He knew nothing about her family, despite his best efforts to dig up the past. And with his connections, his efforts had been pretty damn strong.

"You didn't use science to grow those wings. They came out because that's who you are, Eric."

He couldn't quite wrap his mind around that.

Ella's left hand lifted. She tapped his shoulder. When his gaze turned to her, he found her watching him with sympathy on her face. "This isn't going to be the first time this happens," she said, her voice soft and comforting. "So. Get ready."

He blinked.

She smiled at him. "I told you so."

His jaw dropped.

"I knew what you were, Eric. Even when you didn't." She laughed then and it was such a beautiful, perfect sound. Perfect, just like she was. Not evil. Or dark. Or—

Ella wrapped her arms around him, and he held her tightly. A grin curved his lips because he wouldn't fight it any longer. Maybe they weren't mates. Maybe they were. Didn't really make a difference. She was his heart and that was all that mattered to—

Connor cleared his throat. "You need to know what Cedric told me."

Connor was raining on his parade. Eric growled, "We're transferring him to Purgatory. If that prison won't hold him, death will be the only option."

"Uh, no, that is really *not* an option," Connor responded instantly.

Ella eased away from Eric. He pulled her right back. "Why not?"

Connor slanted a fast glance toward Ella. "Because he said that he did something to her. When he had her in his dungeon. He linked them. According to the bastard we have in containment, if he dies, then so does Ella."

***

"I'm going in," Ella said, her voice flat. "Not you."

Eric forced his back teeth to unclench. "A guy goes a little crazy once..."

"This has always been my fight, Eric. Even if it is one that I thought ended long ago." She squared her shoulders. "I'm talking to Cedric. We're going to find out the truth."

Because maybe the guy was just jerking them around.

And perhaps he wasn't.

"I'll be watching you on the monitor," Eric told her. "He so much as twitches in your direction, and I am in there."

"I'm pretty good at protecting myself, you know. I have my own claws. My own fangs."

He caught her hand in his. Her claws weren't out right then. Eric brought her hand to his lips and pressed a kiss to her palm. "How come you didn't use that strength against me?"

"Because I knew I could reach you."

He kissed her knuckles. "On the surface, some would say that…maybe I'm like him." He had to say those words. "I'm the one who wanted to change. I'm the one who—"

"Tried to keep the world safe? Or decimate every Fey you encountered? Which option did you choose again? Remind me."

His lips thinned. "I started Purgatory."

"And do you put innocents in there?"

"Never." Not on his watch.

"You aren't like him. I can see the difference. I hope you can, too." She pulled her fingers from his and gave a little nod to Connor.

Connor opened Cedric's door.

And Eric watched her walk away.

***

"Ella…" Cedric grinned when he saw her. "Ah, lovely Ella. My Ella." The gold glinted around his ankles and wrists. "Since you're here, I take it that Eric Pate is dead? Tell me that you made him suffer. Tell me that you took your time killing him. I want to hear all the details."

"I'm sure you do." She paused in the middle of the cell. The door had closed behind her. "The compulsion, that was interesting. I'm surprised you managed to control him."

"I can control all vampires *and* werewolves."

"Now you're just bragging."

He laughed. "I am. It took me a while to master that compulsion bit. I had to take more power…more wings."

Damn him.

"But eventually, I was strong enough. I mean, it stands to reason I can control them, right? I helped to make them all."

"And you…connected us."

His face hardened. "We were always connected. You knew that. That was why you became my lover."

"I became your lover because you were dashing. A warrior. Handsome. Strong. I thought I knew you, but when I saw past your mask, I just wanted to run as far and as fast as I could."

He leapt to his feet. The chains stretched but held him in place. "And your Eric?" Cedric spat. "What did you think when you saw past *his* mask? Did you like what you saw?"

She remembered the wildness. The savagery. And the way he hadn't hurt her, even at his absolute worst. "I like the man that he is."

"The *dead* man—"

"No." Ella shook her head. "Want to hear something funny? Eric is actually Fey. And that part of him…it was stronger than your compulsion. Stronger than you. He fought it. He never hurt me. And he's back in control."

Cedric's gaze flew around the cell, then locked on the camera. "Liar!" Cedric screamed. "You aren't stronger than me! They have you in chains, don't they? You're locked up, too! Going to your precious Purgatory, going to—"

"He isn't going to Purgatory. But you will be."

"No, no…*I won't be caged!*"

"The way you caged me? And so many others?" She nodded. "You will be. It seems fitting." Then, deliberately, she turned her back on him.

"When I die, you die."

Ella didn't look back at him. "Why would that be true?"

"Because I made it so."

"I don't think it's possible…"

"It wasn't possible for a man to become Fey, but I did. I took your blood, I gave you mine. I transformed you. I made you weaker, and I made myself stronger…because we *are* linked. I die, then you die."

His words rang with truth. But she didn't understand how he'd made it happen. It shouldn't be possible.

Maybe he is just lying to me. He couldn't have linked us that way.

"Did I ever tell you…" Cedric asked her softly, "about the time I met a djinn? He was part of a traveling crew that came to my land. I didn't believe what he could do at first, so I made a wish."

Her heart drummed faster.

"My first wish was to find a woman of power. A woman who could make me feel like no other."

And you met me. What had he felt for her? A djinn's twisted wish wouldn't have made it love. *Obsession.*

"My second wish was that our lives would be forever entwined. I wanted this power and this woman to be mine for all of my days. So I wished it. I wished that when my heart took its last beat, she wouldn't take another breath."

"That's a damn selfish wish," Ella managed to say through numb lips. Had she met the same djinn that long ago day? She feared that she had. And her wish had been distorted just as Cedric's had.

"I *am* a selfish bastard. Why would I let anyone else take what was mine?"

She looked back at him.

"Do you believe in the power of a djinn?" Cedric asked her. "I did. And I still do…"

Finally, she understood. Cedric hadn't bound them.

Magic had.

***

"Get Olivia in here," Eric snapped. "Right the fuck now."

Because he had far too much experience with djinns. And if Cedric had made that wish…yes, Ella and Cedric would be linked. The end wouldn't be pretty. And the end—it couldn't happen.

Ella had turned to face Cedric now. The bastard looked so smug. So certain. Would Purgatory hold him? Eric honestly wasn't sure, and he couldn't just let the bastard run around loose in the world, killing at will, stalking Ella…

I can't let him be a threat to her.

But he also couldn't kill him.

No one could.

***

"The funny thing about a djinn's wish…" Ella kept her voice totally calm. "Those wishes never work out the way you think. Sure, you can wish for a woman of power but, I'm betting when you made that wish, you never thought that power would consume you. Or that I would. But it happened, right? And you just haven't been the same since."

"You're mine."

She nodded. "That could be the madness of the wish talking. Djinns twist wishes. They give you what you wish for, just not in the way you really wanted." She paused. "So let's be clear on the wording of that second wish. When your heart stops, I don't take another breath…that is what you said, right?"

He gave a jerky nod.

Ella stepped toward him, drawn now because she wouldn't be his prisoner for eternity—and that was what he was trying to make her. "How long do I go without that breath? A minute? An hour?"

His brow furrowed.

"A day? A week?

"Forever!"

"Did you put that in your wish? Because I bet you didn't and that means maybe I won't take another breath for five minutes. Or maybe it will be five years, but then…*maybe* I come back. Maybe I get *another* breath. While you're just growing colder and colder as you face death."

"No!"

***

"What's happening?" Olivia demanded as she rushed toward Eric. "Is Ella all right?"

He grabbed her wrists and pulled her close. "I need you to make a wish."

Her eyes doubled in size. "No, no, I can't do that anymore!" She glanced over her shoulder. Shane was approaching with a hard glare as he saw Eric's tight hold on Olivia. "I'm not a djinn! I changed!"

Because she'd been bitten by her lover. Transformed into a vampire.

Or so Shane had wanted him to believe. But Eric wasn't a fool. He'd been paying attention. Olivia had plenty of bite now, but he didn't think she'd lost her djinn power. At least, not fully.

"You have to make a wish," he said.

"Get your hands off her, Eric!" Shane blasted.

Eric glanced toward the screen. Ella was getting too close to Cedric. "She needs to stand back." His heart pounded faster in his chest. "She can't get too close."

"Let Olivia go!" Shane ordered again.

"Make a wish," Eric said. His gaze was on the screen. On that terrible video feed. And he saw Cedric's claws burst from his fingertips. He saw the bastard get ready to attack—

But Cedric's claws didn't head toward Ella. He sank them into his own chest.

Into his own heart.

"Make a fucking wish!" Eric begged, voice gone hoarse. "Keep her with me!"

Then he was running, kicking in that damn door, and racing into Cedric's containment cell.

Eric's wings burst from his back. He flew across the room. He yanked Cedric's hand out of his chest and broke the bastard's wrist.

Blood poured down Cedric's shirtfront. So much blood. He was choking and laughing. "Won't…go to…your Purgatory…"

Eric tried to stop the blood. He—

Cedric had nearly clawed out his own heart. Sick bastard.

"Without her…" Cedric rasped. "You'll be…one in…Purgatory…living…" Blood poured from his mouth. "Hell…"

And he stilled. Eric had his fingers on the bastard's heart. He was trying to squeeze it. Trying to make that damn thing beat because if it stopped, that would mean that Ella was gone. Ella couldn't be gone. She couldn't. She—

"Eric…"

His head snapped up. She was on the ground, cradled in Olivia's arms. He hadn't even heard the others rush in after him.

Ella had gone pale. Her lips were trembling.

He leapt to her side.

Not her last breath. It can't be. Her heart had to keep beating. She had to keep breathing. She had to stay alive.

"Baby, no, please." And his heart was breaking. Everything was breaking. His life. His world. His mind. She couldn't leave him. They'd just found each other. Too fast. He had to have more time with her. He needed forever with her.

And she wasn't breathing.

Her eyes were still open. Those beautiful eyes. Open and on him. But it was like he was looking into a doll's eyes. There was no emotion there. No life. No *Ella*. She was gone. He touched her neck, but there was no pulse. He put his hand over her chest, but *her heart wasn't beating*.

"No!" His wings snapped back behind him. He jerked Ella out of Olivia's arms. Held her to his chest. "No, come back!" His eyes locked on Olivia's desperate expression. "Wish it!" he ordered. "Wish that she breathes. Wish that she comes back to me."

Pity flashed in Olivia's eyes. "You know my wishes—"

"I don't care!" Eric yelled. "I need her—more than anything." And he bowed over Ella. "I need her. I need…"

Her heart to beat.

"I need her more than life," he said. Then Eric put his mouth on hers. He'd tried to make Cedric's heart keep beating. That had been wrong. He should have been giving Ella breath.

Giving her life.

"I wish..." Eric dimly heard Olivia say. But he was too focused on Ella to hear the rest of Olivia's whispered words.

He breathed for her, pushing air past her lips. Giving her the breath that he had. Once. Twice. A dozen times. He kept breathing for her. He'd give her all that he had. He couldn't let her go. He *couldn't* do it. Nothing had ever mattered more. He wouldn't stop. Not until she came back.

The minutes ticked by.

How long do I go without that breath? A minute? An hour?

He kept breathing for her. Kept giving her air.

Her eyes were open and so heart-breakingly blank. She was too still.

He pressed his lips to hers.

Connor's hand curled over his shoulders. "She's gone. I am so damn sorry, man I—"

"I won't give up on her." He sucked in another gulp of air, then tenderly gave it to Ella. Mouth to mouth. He'd keep it up. "I won't."

He was wrecked on the inside, and he knew his sanity was barely hanging on but he had to—

Ella shuddered in his arms.

It was his turn to stop breathing.

Then he looked into her eyes, and Ella was there. *His* Ella. She stared back at him with life and love and she was *there*.

She was breathing now. Sucking in deep, desperate gulps of air. And he hugged her, pulling her against him and holding on as tightly as he could.

So tight. *Never let go. Never.*

"Eric," she said his name hoarsely. "I was trying to find you. For so long."

And he'd almost lost her. He eased back, just so he could stare into her eyes once again. Just so he could see her. Eric brushed her heavy hair off her forehead. "I fucking love you." She was the one who owned him. Did she realize it? His heart and mind and soul. Everything.

"I know," Ella smiled at him. "I could hear you saying that. I was in the dark and I couldn't find you. But you were in my head. Telling me you loved me…helping me to reach you."

He didn't know what she was talking about, but as long as she was alive, that was all that mattered.

"I love you," Ella told him.

Hell, yes. Yes! Cedric had been wrong. Eric wasn't in hell. He had his Ella. He had a lifetime to spend with her—maybe far longer. Not hell. Not Purgatory.

Paradise.

Heaven.

With Ella.

His forehead pressed to hers, and he held onto her, tighter than he'd ever held on to anyone or anything.

EPILOGUE

When he heard the faint knock at his office door, Eric glanced up. Olivia stood there, biting her lower lip and looking as if she wished she could be anywhere else.

Considering what she was, the woman should be more careful with her wishes.

"Do you have a moment…to talk?" Olivia asked him.

Eric nodded and waved her toward a chair.

"No, I'll just stand. I-I have a patient waiting but I needed you to know…what I wished."

He wasn't sure he wanted to know. "She's alive. She's with me. That's all that matters."

Her hands twisted. "You breathed for her, for over forty-five minutes."

Eric just shrugged. He hadn't been paying attention to time. He'd just been desperate to save her. So desperate that he would have done anything. Even ask a djinn for a wish. Those forty-five minutes had seemed barely longer than a second to him.

"I tried to be careful," she said. "But you know it doesn't really matter how much care I use…"

He waited.

"I almost wished that Ella wouldn't be hurt. But then I thought about how wrong that wish could go. Suddenly her body could be made of stone—something impenetrable so that she'd never feel pain again." She exhaled slowly. "Then I realized that Ella had stopped breathing because she was tied to Cedric. Bound to him. So I wished that she wouldn't be bound to him. Not him. Not anyone."

I was in the dark, and I couldn't find you.

"I don't know if my wish worked or if maybe that was just the way things were supposed to end—she came back and he didn't. Ella was the real Fey, after all. Maybe they are far stronger than anyone realizes."

He knew Ella was strong. No doubt about it.

But he also suspected…she'd chosen. She hadn't been tied by fate or magic to anyone. *She'd* had the choice.

And she'd chosen to come back to him.

Eric cleared his throat. "Thank you, Olivia. I owe you…very much." More than he'd ever be able to repay.

But she shook her head. "No, you don't, Eric. We're friends. Friends don't keep tabs." She turned away and nearly bumped into Lawrence.

No longer under anyone's compulsion, Lawrence had healed. Sure, he might have a wicked new scar, but Eric was damn glad to see his agent back in fighting form once more.

"Thought you'd want to know, boss," Lawrence told him, "the last of Keegan's pack have been transported to Purgatory."

Good. "Thanks, Lawrence. Now why don't you take the night off and get some rest? You sure as hell deserve it." They all did.

Olivia and Lawrence walked away, talking softly. He caught Lawrence's words as they left his room. "I don't know about you, Liv," Lawrence said to her, "but I sure do wish that nothing like this mess with Cedric *ever* happens again."

A faint smile curved his lips. *Be careful what you wish for.* He rather hoped Lawrence didn't get too chatty with Olivia…she might just decide to grant more wishes.

Eric shut down his computer and, a few moments and a quick elevator ride later, he was in front of his apartment. He wouldn't be living in that base much longer. *They* wouldn't be. A place at the base—that wasn't home. He wanted a home with Ella.

A real life.

Before he could open the door, it swung inward. Ella smiled at him. "I've been giving this some thought…" she said. "And I really think I'd make a killer Para Unit Agent."

Her smile was big. Her eyes gleamed. And she truly was his world. "Killer," he agreed, then wrapped his arms around her. He kissed her, and Eric knew he'd waited his whole life for Ella.

And he was so damn lucky that she had found him in the dark.

###

A NOTE FROM THE AUTHOR

I love paranormal stories—anything can happen in them (and it usually does!). It was an absolute pleasure to write DEAL WITH THE DEVIL, and I sure hope that you enjoyed Eric's story. Thank you so much for taking the time to read his book.

If you'd like to stay updated on my releases and sales, please join my newsletter list www.cynthiaeden.com/newsletter/. You can also check out my Facebook page www.facebook.com/cynthiaedenfanpage. I love to post giveaways over at Facebook!

Again, thank you for reading DEAL WITH THE DEVIL.

Best,

Cynthia Eden
www.cynthiaeden.com

If you enjoyed DEAL WITH THE DEVIL, check out the other Purgatory books…

THE WOLF WITHIN (BOOK 1)

Don't miss the other books in the Purgatory series.

FBI Special Agent Duncan McGuire spends his days–and his nights–tracking real-life monsters. Most humans aren't aware of the vampires and werewolves that walk among them. They don't realize the danger that they face, but Duncan knows about the horror that waits in the darkness. He hunts the monsters, and he protects the innocent. Duncan just never expects to become a monster. But after a brutal werewolf attack, Duncan begins to change…and soon he will be one of the very beasts that he has hunted.

Dr. Holly Young is supposed to help Duncan during his transition. It's her job to keep him sane so that Duncan can continue working with the FBI's Para Unit. But as Duncan's beast grows stronger, the passion that she and Duncan have held carefully in check pushes to the surface. The desire that is raging between them could be a very dangerous thing…because Holly isn't exactly human, not any longer.

As the monsters circle in, determined to take out all of the agents working at the Para Unit, Holly and Duncan will have to use their own supernatural strengths in order to survive. But as they give up more of their humanity and embrace the beasts within them both, they realize that the passion between them isn't safe, it isn't controllable, and their dark need may just be an obsession that could destroy them both.

MARKED BY THE VAMPIRE (BOOK 2)

Vampires exist. So do werewolves. The creatures that you fear in the darkness? They're all real. And the baddest of the paranormals…those who love to hurt humans…they're sent to Purgatory, the only paranormal prison in the U.S.

His job is to stop the monsters.

Deadly forces are at work within Purgatory. The monsters are joining together—and their plans have to be stopped. FBI Agent Shane August, a very powerful vampire with a dark past, is sent into the prison on an undercover assignment. His job is to infiltrate the vampire clan, by any means necessary.

She wants to help the prisoners.

Dr. Olivia Maddox wants to find out just why certain paranormals go bad. What pushes some vampires over the edge? Why do some werewolves turn so savage? If she can understand the monsters, then Olivia thinks she can help them. When she gets permission to enter Purgatory, Olivia believes she is being given the research opportunity of a lifetime.

Olivia doesn't realize that she's walking straight into hell.

To survive, they have to rely on each other.

When the prisoners break loose, there is only one person—one vampire—who can protect her, but as Olivia and Shane fight the enemies that surround them, a dark and dangerous passion stirs to life between the doctor and the vamp. Shane realizes that Olivia is a woman carrying secrets—powerful, sinful secrets. Secrets that a man would kill to possess.

And Olivia realizes that—sometimes—you can't control the beast inside of you. No matter how hard you try. Some passions can push you to the very limits of your control…and the growing lust that she feels for her vampire…it's sending her racing right into a deadly storm of desire.

Welcome to Purgatory…a place that's a real hell on earth…

CHARMING THE BEAST (BOOK 3)

He's a man with a beast inside…

Connor Marrok never intended to work for the Seattle Para Unit. He's not one of the good guys—he's a real monster, and the beast he carries doesn't exactly play nicely. But now he finds himself being blackmailed into a new assignment. It's supposed to be his last gig. His mission? Protect the beautiful Chloe Quick. Keep her alive. Destroy her enemies. Easy enough…until he starts to fall for Chloe.

She just wants to escape.

Chloe is tired of being a prisoner. She wants to get away from her Para Unit guard and run fast into the night. So what if Connor is the sexiest guy she's ever met? Chloe knows trouble when she sees it, and Connor is one big, dangerous package of *trou□le*. But, when an obsessed werewolf begins stalking Chloe, she realizes that her paranormal bodyguard may just be the one man she needs the most.

Their attraction is primal.

Every moment that Chloe and Connor spend together increases their attraction. Chloe has never felt a need so strong or a desire so dark. The beast that Chloe carries inside has always been silent, but Connor is stirring up her animal instincts. And as the danger and desire begin to twist together, Chloe wonders just how far she'd be willing to go…in order to spend one more night in Connor's arms.

ABOUT THE AUTHOR

Award-winning author Cynthia Eden writes dark tales of paranormal romance and romantic suspense. Cynthia is a two-time finalist for the RITA® award (she was a finalist both in the romantic suspense category and in the paranormal romance category). Since she began writing full-time in 2005, Cynthia has written over thirty novels and novellas.

Cynthia is a southern girl who loves horror movies, chocolate, and happy endings. More information about Cynthia and her books may be found at: http://www.cynthiaeden.com or on her Facebook page at: http://www.facebook.com/cynthiaedenfanpage. Cynthia is also on Twitter at http://www.twitter.com/cynthiaeden.

HER WORKS

Paranormal romances by Cynthia Eden:

- BOUND BY BLOOD (Bound, Book 1)
- BOUND IN DARKNESS (Bound, Book 2)
- BOUND IN SIN (Bound, Book 3)
- BOUND BY THE NIGHT (Bound, Book 4)
- *FOREVER BOUND - An anthology containing: BOUND BY BLOOD, BOUND IN DARKNESS, BOUND IN SIN, AND BOUND BY THE NIGHT
- BOUND IN DEATH (Bound, Book 5)
- THE WOLF WITHIN (Purgatory, Book 1)
- MARKED BY THE VAMPIRE (Purgatory, Book 2)
- CHARMING THE BEAST (Purgatory, Book 3)

Other paranormal romances by Cynthia Eden:

- A VAMPIRE'S CHRISTMAS CAROL
- BLEED FOR ME
- BURN FOR ME (Phoenix Fire, Book 1)
- ONCE BITTEN, TWICE BURNED (Phoenix Fire, Book 2)

- PLAYING WITH FIRE (Phoenix Fire, Book 3)
- ANGEL OF DARKNESS (Fallen, Book 1)
- ANGEL BETRAYED (Fallen, Book 2)
- ANGEL IN CHAINS (Fallen, Book 3)
- AVENGING ANGEL (Fallen, Book 4)
- IMMORTAL DANGER
- NEVER CRY WOLF
- A BIT OF BITE (Free Read!!)
- ETERNAL HUNTER (Night Watch, Book 1)
- I'LL BE SLAYING YOU (Night Watch, Book 2)
- ETERNAL FLAME (Night Watch, Book 3)
- HOTTER AFTER MIDNIGHT (Midnight, Book 1)
- MIDNIGHT SINS (Midnight, Book 2)
- MIDNIGHT'S MASTER (Midnight, Book 3)
- WHEN HE WAS BAD (anthology)
- EVERLASTING BAD BOYS (anthology)
- BELONG TO THE NIGHT (anthology)

List of Cynthia Eden's romantic suspense titles:

- WATCH ME (Dark Obsession, Book 1)
- WANT ME (Dark Obsession, Book 2)
- NEED ME (Dark Obsession, Book 3)
- MINE TO TAKE (Mine, Book 1)
- MINE TO KEEP (Mine, Book 2)
- MINE TO HOLD (Mine, Book 3)

- MINE TO CRAVE (Mine, Book 4)
- MINE TO HAVE (Mine, Book 5)
- FIRST TASTE OF DARKNESS
- SINFUL SECRETS
- DIE FOR ME (For Me, Book 1)
- FEAR FOR ME (For Me, Book 2)
- SCREAM FOR ME (For Me, Book 3)
- DEADLY FEAR (Deadly, Book 1)
- DEADLY HEAT (Deadly, Book 2)
- DEADLY LIES (Deadly, Book 3)
- ALPHA ONE (Shadow Agents, Book 1)
- GUARDIAN RANGER (Shadow Agents, Book 2)
- SHARPSHOOTER (Shadow Agents, Book 3)
- GLITTER AND GUNFIRE (Shadow Agents, Book 4)
- UNDERCOVER CAPTOR (Shadow Agents, Book 5)
- THE GIRL NEXT DOOR (Shadow Agents, Book 6)
- EVIDENCE OF PASSION (Shadow Agents, Book 7)
- WAY OF THE SHADOWS (Shadow Agents, Book 8)

Printed in Poland
by Amazon Fulfillment
Poland Sp. z o.o., Wrocław